THE MEXICAN GIRL

N.K. CHAVUSH

N.K. CHAVUSH was born in Lambeth, London. He went to school in Somerset and then later to university in Canterbury, where he graduated with a BSc (hons) degree in radiography. He currently resides in Cyprus, with his wife, son and daughter.

www.nkchavush.com

facebook.com/nkchavush

Instagram: n.k.chavush_author

Twitter: @nkchavush

Acknowledgements

Special thanks are in order: To my good friend and editor, Simon
Thompson. Not only has he done a fantastic job editing and proofreading,
but he has also been a great mentor.
Hillary Cinar, for the valuable test reading and insight into Mexican
culture.
Bilge and Fuat Sami for their advice on the book description.
Also, to my loving family, who are always there for me.
And, of course, my beautiful wife, Simay, for making me look good in the
author's photo and for being so supportive of this novel.

This book is dedicated to my father,

Mehmet Chavush

1

THE first time Inspector Nicolas Kean met Daniela Flores was the night she walked into the police station, drenched from the October rain. Although it was Halloween, she was one of the few students not in costume having fun in one of the many pubs in town. She came in to report a missing person—a boy she'd been dating for a couple of weeks.

Constable Reading, from the front desk, called Inspector Kean's office phone after taking her details to check whether further questioning was necessary. Canterbury was swarming with students, so there were occasional cases where someone had vanished—at least for a short period. However, the crime rate was generally low.

'When was he last seen?' asked Kean—referring to the missing person—as he sluggishly stretched back in the chair.

'She claims he's been missing for three days. He hasn't been to work since Thursday, and his roommates haven't seen him for a while either.'

'How about family members? Next of kin?'

'Victor is Portuguese. His family lives in Lisbon. He works at the Texan Chicken Bar on the High Street.'

'I see. Show her into Room 2,' replied Kean, taking a sip of his lukewarm coffee. 'What's her name?'

And that was the first time he heard her name—an indirect introduction that would undoubtedly change the rest of his life forever.

'Daniela Flores,' answered the Constable.

What an exquisite name. These Latin names have a certain charm about them, thought Kean.

'Spanish?'

'Mexican,' corrected the Constable.

Opening a new page in his notebook, the Inspector jotted down the missing person details—*Victor Silva. Aged 24.*

Nationality, Portuguese. Missing. Last seen: Texan Chicken Bar, Canterbury, Thursday, October 28th. Reported by Daniela Flores. Aged 22.

Coffee in hand, he headed to Room 2 and pushed the door open—and there she was, quietly sitting in deep thought on the other side of the table. Albeit pale with worry, she still looked beautiful, with high cheekbones, perfectly shaped nose and lips—and long shiny black hair almost reaching down to her waist. Her large brown eyes looked up at Kean as he walked in. The heavy door whacked him from behind, causing him to jerk forward and spill two large splats of coffee all over his white shirt.

'*Shit!*'

Talking about making a fool of myself and also swearing out loud …very professional! He thought.

He couldn't tell whether she was holding back her laughter or if she was genuinely concerned for her missing friend. But all the same, she managed to keep a straight face as he sat down and wiped his shirt with a crumpled-up tissue that he dug out of his trouser pocket.

'Apologies for swearing. I don't usually—'

'It's okay,' she said hoarsely, averting her eyes and looking down at the table instead.

'Would you like a cup?'

'No, thanks.'

'So, your boyfriend?' asked Kean, placing himself down opposite her.

'He isn't my boyfriend. We only just started dating a couple of weeks ago.'

'And has it been three days since he was last seen?'

'Yes, maybe a bit longer,' she sniffed.

She looked deep into Kean's eyes. Caught off guard by her sheer beauty and seductive glance—he felt his jaw drop.

'I see,' he said, clearing his throat. 'And did he ever mention going anywhere? Maybe away to see a friend or a relative or anything like that?'

She shook her head. 'He doesn't have many friends.'

'Does he live alone?' asked Kean.

'He lives with three other tenants. The two boys are students, and the girl is one of their girlfriends. Victor doesn't really mix with them much.'

'I'd like to talk to them.'

Daniela shrugged. 'Alright.'

Kean tried to examine her every move. *Even the most innocent looking people can be guilty—and they often are,* he thought. But it was hard to tell with Daniela. She would be a hard nut to crack. She had a mysterious essence about her.

Pressing her phone on, she passed it over to him. 'This is Victor.'

He examined the picture—a selfie of them snuggling.

'Can you send me that?'

'Sure.'

He gave her his number.

'Are you a student?' he asked.

'I am.'

'What do you study?'

'I'm doing a master's in Political Science,' she replied.

'And how about Victor?'

'He's not a student. He came here to work.'

'Okay… and how was your last date?'

She was thoughtful for a moment.

'Actually, not good. We argued.'

'Argued?'

There was another moment's silence. Kean waited for more, but she just kept quiet, reliving the argument as her face turned slightly red.

'What did you argue about?' pushed Kean.

Daniela smiled slightly and let out a somewhat frustrated laugh, her pure white straight teeth shining brightly under the interrogation room's spotlight.

'He had a problem with his father. They weren't talking. He kept ignoring his calls.'

'What was the problem?'

'It was none of my business, really, but I just can't help poking my nose into other people's lives. His parents had a big argument, and his father left home. That's all I know. I told him that he should talk to him at least. But he told me that it was nothing to do with me and that I should stop being so nosey.'

Kean took a deep breath and rubbed his eyes.

It wouldn't look good if a missing person's report said the couple had a quarrel, and shortly after, one of them went missing. Even though it might not have really been an argument that would have harmed their relationship, it could be relevant because he was missing. She has innocent written all over her face, thought Kean—*and God! Isn't it angelic?*

'Do you think that's the reason why he disappeared?' he asked.

Daniela shook her head. 'No. He wouldn't just disappear because of that.'

'Or, maybe, as his parents are having problems, he went to visit his family?'

'He was saving up to go there for Christmas. He would have notified his work first,' explained Daniela.

Then there was that moment—it was only for a couple of seconds or so, but it seemed to last a lifetime. They stared into each other's eyes and said nothing. Daniela's face lit up, and Kean could have sworn that behind the bitterness and anxiety hid a glimmer of a smile—even if it was just his imagination.

'Rest assured, Miss Flores. We will do everything we can to track him down!' he said with a deep sigh, breaking his gaze.

'That's very reassuring. Thank you, Inspector—?'

Damn! Really? Haven't I introduced myself? He thought, feeling like an idiot.

'I'm Inspector Nicolas Kean.'

This time, she really did raise a smile and nodded.

Kean told her that he would update her on any developments. She thanked him, then left, not looking too hopeful that Victor would be found.

When he returned to his office, he started the investigation process immediately. He decided to check Daniela's Facebook profile. Even the slightest clue could turn out to be something big and play a vital role in solving a case. But all he found were a couple of old selfies with her friends, taken in London. The profile was mainly set as private. Apart from learning that her birthday was October 5ᵗʰ and that she was highly photogenic, he found nothing useful—not for the investigation anyway.

He also checked Victor's account. There were thousands of Victor Silvas. He tried to compare the profile photos with the one Daniela had sent him, but none of them matched.

He brought up the name X on his mobile and pressed the call button, feeling a rush of adrenaline running through his veins. As much as he tried, he just couldn't get Daniela out of his mind. He'd always been professional at work when it came to relationships, and he intended to keep it that way. But soon, all that would change.

X was an outlaw—a rogue—and an ex-soldier who once worked for the MI5 before getting his licence confiscated. But as far as Kean was concerned, he was a reliable source—someone Kean trusted would get some information from the streets and maybe shed some light on unanswered questions whenever a dead end was reached. X owed Kean his life. If it wasn't for Kean, he would be rotting away in a dark cell. Although Kean would provide X with a commission when he gave him any helpful information—usually in an envelope that he'd leave on a small round table at The Cathedral Café—he preferred to remain anonymous. He had no face or name—

a ghost in the shadows. Kean had no idea what X looked like. He'd blend into the overcrowded cafe, sweeping past the table in a long cream coloured coat, dark shades and a hat so Kean wouldn't notice him, or the envelope disappearing. The only thing that did stick in Kean's memory was a silver keyring in the shape of a cross with the letters SR engraved on it that he once saw hanging out of the pocket of his cream-coloured coat before he disappeared into the crowd.

'I need some information on two residents from Canterbury,' said Kean.

'Sure, give me their names,' replied X in a husky distorted voice.

'Victor Silva, aged twenty-four …missing. And Daniela Flores, twenty-two. Flores reported Silva *as* missing. I want a background check on them both …anything that might not show up on the police files.'

'Leave it with me, Inspector,' he said coldly before hanging up.

2

RON poured the last of the cornflakes into the cracked bowl, shaking the packet to loosen the remaining particles stuck at the bottom. He then opened the fridge, hoping there was some milk left.

'I say we call the police. I don't trust that bitch,' said Julie as she sat smoking with a shaky hand.

'She's not that bad. Great, no fucking milk left! How can I eat my cereal with only two bloody drops!?'

'Stop whining, you idiot! And you're only sayin' that coz you fancy her,' mocked Julie.

'Well, she *is* hot. Bet you wouldn't say no either,' spat Ron, while crunching on a mouthful of cornflakes.

'You're sick! So, are you gonna call the police or not? We need to inform them about Victor!'

'Daniela probably informed them already …okay, don't look at me like that. I'll do it! I don't see why you can't do it, though.'

'What? With my reputation? It's better that *you* talk to them!' replied Julie while dismissively gazing out of the window.

They looked questioningly at each other when the doorbell rang. They weren't used to having visitors—especially this early in the morning. Rash's heavy footsteps could be heard stomping down the stairs.

Rash opened the door slightly and poked his face between the gap, observing a man with sleek black hair and green eyes waiting outside.

'Good morning, I'm Nicolas Kean. I'm with the CID, investigating the disappearance of a Mr Victor Silva. I would like to ask you some questions. May I come in?' said Kean, flashing his badge.

On seeing this, Rash's facial expression changed while he examined the badge. 'Sure,' he said, unlocking the chain and scratching the back of his head as Kean walked in.

Inside, a cocktail of smoke, alcohol, and body odour hit Kean. The curtains were drawn, and it was evident that the house hadn't been ventilated for a while.

He followed Rash into the kitchen, where Julie and Ron were. Julie shot him a look and winced slightly as she kept smoke in her lungs before uncontrollably exhaling it without breaking her gaze.

Ron cleared his throat and carefully placed the bowl of cereal on the table while still chewing, not taking his eyes off Kean.

'A missing person has been reported who resides at this address. A Victor Silva.'

'We were actually going to report Victor as missing today,' admitted Ron.

'His girlfriend—I mean, a girl he was dating, Daniela Flores, beat you to it.'

No one said a word.

'When was the last time you saw Silva?' Kean added, carefully examining each of the housemates. They kept still with their heads bowed, like schoolkids in the headmaster's office who were just about to receive a detention.

'I actually can't remember when, but he works long hours. And when he's not at work, he's usually hanging out with the Mexican bird,' explained Ron while Julie nodded with approval. 'We thought Victor might have been cotching with her.'

'He was hardly here. And even when he was, he's not the kind of person you'd notice,' stated Julie somewhat sarcastically, extinguishing her cigarette in an ashtray filled with many other fag-ends.

'A quiet person,' Rash interrupted, stroking his long beard.

'Tell me about Daniela Flores,' said Kean.

All three looked at each other.

'They only met a couple of weeks ago. She hardly talked to us,' explained Ron.

'She seems nice,' added Rash, receiving an awkward look from the other two.

'Can I take a quick look at Mr Silva's room?' asked Kean.

All three shrugged. 'Sure.'

Kean's first impression was that nothing about Victor's housemates indicated that they were involved in his disappearance. Typical university students stuck in their own world, no doubt breathing the air of freedom after leaving school.

Victor's room was untidy—a typical student zone with crumpled up empty coke cans and crisps packets scattered all over the place. A dusty medium-sized suitcase was resting on top of the cupboard. Victor certainly didn't go away on holiday. The Inspector searched the closet and the drawers. There weren't many clothes either. Sadly, he couldn't find any evidence.

Just as Kean was making his way down the stairs to leave, Sergeant John O'Leary called. A body had been found, washed up on the shore in Whitstable, some ten miles away from Canterbury. The Inspector rushed to the scene to check it out.

'There doesn't seem to be any foul play,' explained Sergeant O'Leary, standing back and watching the forensic team collect samples. At the same time, the paramedics were waiting to take the body away. 'But then again, can't be too sure until the autopsy report is out.

'Indeed. So, you reckon he drowned?' Kean asked, placing his cold hands into the warmth of his jacket pockets.

'It's hard to tell, really. If it was my guess, I'd say he was either pushed or fell off a boat. Unless he got so drunk that he decided to go for a swim.'

'In the middle of the winter, fully clothed?'

'We'll test the body for any alcohol or drugs,' explained O'Leary. 'But as I said, there doesn't seem to be any foul play.'

'Please contact me asap when you get the results from the autopsy.'

'Will do, Inspector.'

Just as Kean turned to walk back to the car, his phone rang. The number was withheld, and right away, he guessed who it was. Watching the paramedics place the black body bag into the back of an ambulance, he answered.

'Inspector, I have some interesting information,' said X's voice at the other end.

He paced further away from Sergeant O'Leary.

'I'm listening,' he said, feeling the breeze from the sea on the back of his neck as seagulls screeched noisily from above.

'I take it that you have no idea who Daniela Flores is,' said X almost mockingly.

'She's a student of Mexican origin, studying at the Canterbury University College.'

'Right. She also happens to be the daughter of the Mexican Ambassador to London.'

Kean remained silent for a moment and could feel himself take a deep, uncomfortable sigh.

'You're joking,' he said.

X replied. 'Since when have I had a sense of humour?'

'So, now I have a dead body washed up on the shore and a girl who's the Mexican Ambassador's daughter, who reported the victim as missing!'

X forced out a slight laugh. 'Good luck, Inspector.'

3

DANIELA and Inspector Kean looked deep into each other's eyes. Her gaze was glassy, and her eyes were red. He felt sorry for her. It's never easy to tell people that someone close to them has passed, even if they'd only dated for a couple of weeks.

'It doesn't make sense,' she said, wiping a tear from her cheek.

'Death never does,' Kean said.

'He didn't even know how to swim, so what was he doing in the water?'

'*What?*'

'He mentioned it before when we were talking about the summer holidays. I found it quite amusing. Someone from Portugal who can't swim is unheard of.'

'So, if he couldn't swim, then why did he end up in the sea with clothes on, in the middle of winter?' questioned Kean.

Daniela looked deeper into his eyes and held tightly onto his gaze. A look he tried not to invite, but all the same, it made his heart beat faster. As she went into deep thought, she played with her perfectly straight, shiny black hair. Kean sensed that there was a mutual feeling between them. Something that he had to shut out—but deep down he knew that he couldn't. And then again, he knew damn well it was unethical even to think about what they were both feeling.

'What did your family think of your relationship with Victor?' he asked, hoping that she'd tell him who her father was.

'As I mentioned before, we hadn't been dating long. They didn't know about Victor,' she explained, looking away, contemplating whether to say more …but she didn't.

Kean's phone rang and startled them both. O'Leary's name flashed on the screen.

Kean answered.

'We're now looking at a possible homicide,' said O'Leary with a level of excitement in his voice. Kean knew that although most of the police wouldn't admit it …they feel a certain energy—a buzz when a case turns out to be murder.

'How come?' he asked O'Leary.

'Rohypnol was found in Victor's system, along with alcohol. Meaning that his drink was spiked! This explains why he was alive when he entered the water. Probably didn't know what he was doing!'

'Unbelievable!' exclaimed Kean in shock.

'Shall I bring you the report, Inspector?'

'Yes, please do, O'Leary. Thank you.'

Kean hung up and turned his attention back to Daniela, who seemed curious about O'Leary's call.

'Is there anything at all you're not telling me?' he asked, turning up the heat.

He could see that the question irritated her. She looked anxious all of a sudden and crossed her arms together and frowned.

'No. I told you everything. I'm not hiding anything!'

'I don't doubt that. Except we are now dealing with a murder case.'

'Murder?'

'That's right! And whoever did it is a real professional. They knew exactly what they were doing to make it look like an accident!'

Suddenly, she started to sob. Kean handed her a tissue and tried not to let his feelings get in the way. He waited for a moment and took a deep breath. 'Why didn't you say before who your father is?' he asked.

Taken aback, she shot him an odd look and sighed.

'It's not something I advertise,' she breathed.

'Are you sure that your family didn't know about Silva?'

'What are you implying, Inspector? No, they didn't know!'

'I have to look at all possibilities,' explained Kean somewhat apologetically.

She nodded.

They both stopped and looked into each other's eyes again. She was just about to say something when there was a knock at the door. O'Leary walked in and introduced himself to Daniela. By the look on his face, Kean could see that O'Leary was also quite struck by her beauty. He handed over the autopsy report, with a slight grin on his face.

'I'm sorry for your loss,' he told her.

She raised a slight smile welcoming his condolence.

'If and when there are any new developments, we will contact you,' the Inspector told Daniela. 'Don't go too far.'

'I won't,' she replied.

'I know what you're thinking, Sergeant, and it's unethical!' Kean said to O'Leary.

O'Leary laughed. 'Can't be helped, Inspector! She's a stunner.'

Kean let out a laugh. 'What are you like? Seriously!'

He made his way to his office, eagerly scanning the autopsy report. The death was caused by asphyxiation. Victor had definitely drowned. There was nothing physical …no foul play. A small amount of alcohol was found in the victim's system—not enough to get him drunk. However, the biggest surprise was the Rohypnol— a drug commonly used by rapists to spike their victim's drink. But the crucial question was: *How did it end up in the victim's body?*

Kean called Dr Osman Gami for advice. He was the pathologist who had performed the autopsy.

'A small trace of Rohypnol was present in the bladder. You see, Inspector, Rohypnol leaves the body fast and is therefore sometimes extremely hard to detect. So just to be sure, I did a hair follicle test, which gives a more accurate reading up to thirty days after death. And the answer to your question is, yes, the victim's beer was spiked.'

Thanking Dr Gami, Kean hung up. It wasn't long before he received another call. To his surprise, it was Rash, Victor's housemate.

'Inspector Kean? I'm not sure how important this is, but you did say if there's anything else, we should let you know.'

'Yes, what is it?'

'After hearing that Victor had been killed—'

'It's not definite that he was killed, but we're looking into it.'

'Well ...I always felt uncomfortable about the large man who hangs around Daniela. Do you think he had anything to do with it?'

'What man?'

There was a moment's silence.

'Oh, I thought that you knew. He is like some kind of bodyguard or something,' explained Rash.

'Are you sure?' asked the Inspector, jotting the new information down in his notebook.

'Yes. He always used to stand outside, looking up at the window whenever Daniela came to the house to see Victor. The guy always gave me the creeps.'

Daniela was caught off guard when Kean called, just as she was about to attend a lecture.

'Why didn't you mention that you have a bodyguard?' he asked her sternly.

'I don't think you understand the protocol, Inspector. I'm not permitted to discuss with anyone the fact that I'm under protection …or who my father is!' she whispered sharply.

'Listen! Someone is dead, and up until now, the only suspect is you. Now I find out you have a bodyguard! So, I don't care about your protocol, Miss Flores!'

'What do you want from me?'

'I want to have a chat with your bodyguard.'

She puffed her cheeks with acrimony and looked across to the other end of the courtyard at the large figure who was always carefully watching her every move.

'Fine, my lecture finishes in an hour. We'll be at the police station in two,' she said.

4

HE sat with a blank expression on his face, suggesting that interrogating him would be a waste of time. His bald head perfectly reflected the light shining from the spotlight above, and the scar running from under his right eye down his cheek was as equally as prominent. He was a big man—who easily had an extra foot advantage in height over Kean, and at least ten kilos in weight. He had been sent over from Mexico to work primarily at the Mexican Embassy in London. Although his name was Jose Perez, Daniela (who was waiting in the hall outside) referred to him as Jack. She wasn't too happy about him talking to the police either.

'My job is to make sure Daniela is safe! Not to kill people she makes friends with!' explained Jack, unaware that soon things would get out of control.

O'Leary shot Kean a look. This was certainly not the typical interrogation they were used to doing.

'And have you killed before?' asked Kean scanning previous pages through in his notebook.

Jack exhaled and slightly nodded, uneasy about the question.

'As a matter of fact, yes, I have. I served in the Mexican army. I was involved with the Zapatista Uprising.'

His mind began to drift as he closed his eyes, reliving bullets whizzing past him and the deafening bombs shaking the ground as debris rained down. And then there was the wounded, the dying, and the dead—most of them decapitated and covered in blood.

'It couldn't have been easy,' is all O'Leary could think to say.

Kean kept quiet, giving Jack a moment to compose himself. Opening his eyes, he looked at O'Leary, then locked eyes with the Inspector.

'No war is easy,' Jack whispered harshly. 'In fact, I can't think of anything worse. Especially, civil war.'

'And your family?' Kean asked.

Jack shook his head as his face turned grim and his eyes watery. 'My wife and son …the war,' he stuttered, unable to finish the sentence. 'They were caught in the crossfire—'

Then he fell silent and sank into deep thought again.

O'Leary gave him a sympathetic look. What Jack had said hit him hard, being a father himself.

'I'm sorry to hear that,' said Kean.

O'Leary was just about to speak but stopped himself and rolled his eyes. Two female police officers could be heard walking past the interrogation room, chatting and laughing loudly. After they were gone, O'Leary asked Jack what he thought of Victor Silva.

'You want me to be honest? Or lie and tell you what a great guy he was? I have to warn you that I'm always upfront and frank.'

'We always want to know the truth,' Kean said with a slight smile.

'What can I say? The guy loved himself. And you know what? Although Miss Flores couldn't see it, it was blatantly obvious that he was after a free ticket home!'

'And did you approach her about this?' asked O'Leary.

'I'm her bodyguard, not her financial advisor!' replied Jack.

'Would you say he was a danger to her?' Kean asked.

Jack thought for a moment. 'Not really. Not in a physical way anyway.'

Suddenly, O'Leary started to lose his cool.

'Listen, if you're hiding anything, you need to tell us now! If we find out later that you're keeping things from us, we won't be as nice as we are now!'

Jack stared at O'Leary blankly.

'I—'

'Come on! It was you, wasn't it?' pushed O'Leary, trying to break Jack.

'Sergeant!' Kean cut in, trying to calm him.

'You just wanted to scare him but ended up killing him, didn't you? Admit it!' hissed O'Leary.

'As I said before, I am *not* a murderer,' Jack said calmly. 'Now, if you excuse me, I'd like to go.'

'In that case, I'm sure you or Miss Flores wouldn't mind if we checked both your homes,' said Kean.

'Sure. Be my guest!' answered Jack without hesitation.

After he left, the look on O'Leary's face was grim. He clicked his pen a couple of times looking irritated.

'What do you think, Inspector? Do you think he's involved?'

'To be honest, O'Leary, no, I don't,' admitted the Inspector.

'You sound very sure.'

'He has strict orders to make sure Miss Flores is safe. He wouldn't risk spiking someone's drink, then take them all the way to Whitstable. It just doesn't make sense.'

'Unless Miss Flores is also involved, somehow,' said O'Leary.

'Which is why their homes must be searched.'

'This place is too luxurious for student accommodation,' Sergeant Peter Rickson said, perhaps a bit too loudly.

O'Leary was busy with other duties, so the Inspector was accompanied by Rickson instead. Daniela stayed on the top floor of the rented maisonette, with the bottom floor reserved for Jack.

A maid waiting at the front door greeted them.

'Please remove your shoes before entering,' she demanded.

Peter gave Kean an odd look. 'Really?' he mumbled under his breath.

As they removed their shoes, Daniela materialised at the top of the staircase.

'Let's get this over and done with,' she said. Since Kean had seen her at the station earlier, she had changed into a dark green t-shirt and jeans. She looked stunning, with an athletic figure, her jeans perfectly wrapped around her hips. She turned and led the way with the two policemen following.

They searched the bedroom first. The bed was a king-sized mahogany with matching cupboards on either side and other luxury furniture—like a princess's bedroom out of a fairy tale.

A large safe was concealed at the back of one of the cupboards, obstructed by a curtain of Daniela's hanging coats and long dresses.

'Can we take a look inside?' asked Kean, giving Daniela a slightly sympathetic look.

She puffed her cheeks. 'Do I have a choice?' she asked.

'We'll be quick,' he said.

She asked them to turn around so she could enter the code. When Kean turned, he noticed Jack standing at the doorway with a frown on his face, like some bouncer guarding a cheap nightclub. The safe door beeped and clicked open.

'Done,' said Daniela, standing back, but eyeing the safe like a lioness ready to pounce on its prey.

Inside, the safe was divided into two compartments. The top was occupied by jewellery—mostly diamonds. And the bottom was stacked with fifty-pound notes. Sergeant Rickson's jaw dropped.

'And how much cash is in here exactly?' Kean asked as he knelt down, lifting some of the stacks and checking for anything hidden underneath.

'About twenty thousand,' replied Daniela.

The Inspector looked up at her. 'Don't you have a bank account?' he asked, getting back up.

His question was met with a slight nod, but no reply.

'Right. You can close the safe.' he said to Daniela.

After looking through the medicine cupboard in the kitchen and through the drawers, there seemed to be nothing out of the ordinary. Although Rickson was young, keen and couldn't wait to make his first arrest, Kean knew they were barking up the wrong tree.

Next, they searched Jack's maisonette downstairs, which was in no way as glamourous compared with Daniela's one above. In fact, it was extremely plain with hardly any furniture or even a TV. There was just one single bed, a cupboard, and a small table in the kitchen. One thing that was particularly striking was a framed picture on the kitchen table of his wife and boy, who was a spitting image of Jack.

Every night they'd watch Jack eat his ready-made dinner and then he'd have a couple of beers while chatting to them.

'I know if you were here, you'd make me something better than this,' he used to say—and it's as if she'd smile and agree but then disapprove when he drank those can of beers.

As for his son—he'd just smile …and always kept smiling. I love you Daddy.

The two policemen thanked Daniela and Jack for allowing them to perform a quick search of their homes. Nothing had been found. No clues. No evidence. Again, the case had turned cold.

5

THREE weeks passed, and to the locals, the tragic death of Victor Silva was long forgotten. And who could have blamed them? Victor was a foreigner with no family in town and hardly any friends. For a while, there was some speculation on how he died. This wasn't a typical murder case—if it was actually a murder at all.

Victor's death might have indeed been erased from the locals' minds, but for Nicolas Kean, it was the only thing he could think about. Especially now that it had reached a dead end. He had spent hours watching CCTV footage, but unfortunately, only a few cameras covered the Whitstable area.

Occasionally, Daniela would call, asking about any new developments, but there weren't any, and the body had already been sent to Lisbon for Victor's grieving family to bury. The conversations never lasted long. They would always end the same way, with her thanking him.

Like most Monday afternoons, Daniela was studying in the college library. She always worked hard and aimed to achieve the highest marks. Her mother used to say that she was overly ambitious, just like her father. On this occasion, she was writing an essay on human rights when Harry Barnes, an occupational therapy student, approached her, gawking at her with his large staring eyes. Rash, who also happened to be there, watched from the level above as he sat in the inner terrace and occasionally scanned the quiet library.

'Hello Daniel,' Harry said.

Hesitantly, Daniela quickly glimpsed at Jack, sitting at the other end of the library, and shook her head.

Everything's cool.

'Harry ...how've you been?'

'Same old, my darling. And yourself?'

'Yeah, good.'

'Great!'

'So, how about a drink tonight?' Harry asked out of the blue.

'Wow, I dunno. It feels a bit too soon to be dating.'

'Dating? I only asked if you wanted to join me for a drink,' laughed Harry. 'Come on. It'll be good for you. Take your mind off things.'

'Alright, just a quick one,' said Daniela relenting.

Harry raised a smile. 'Excellent, see you at the White Owl at nine,' he said, checking his worn-out digital watch, strapped loosely around his wrist.

After he left, Daniela tried to focus on her essay but seemed to have lost her flow after the distraction from Harry. She noticed a shadow standing beside her. It was Rash.

'Rash, hello,' she said with a friendly smile.

'Hello Daniela,' he replied. 'You never come over anymore.'

'I know. Although Victor and I weren't seeing each other for that long, there are still memories.'

Rash sighed. 'Yeah, I know.'

Daniela looked lost, not sure what else to say.

'Be careful. He's a player,' explained Rash, looking in the direction that Harry Barnes had gone. 'The library is his hunting ground.'

Daniela let out a slight laugh. 'Thanks, Rash. I'll bear that in mind.'

'I'll see you around,' he said to her, shooting an uncomfortable look at Jack and swallowing hard.

Daniela couldn't believe she'd agreed to go on a date with Harry. Just what was she thinking? She was now even more distracted after talking to Rash. She stared outside. It was getting dark, and she watched the tiny spatters of rain striking the window becoming more and more intense. Looking at the time, she panicked slightly. It was 17:25.

The library shut at six, and she hadn't done as much writing as she had hoped. And to make matters worse, she was going out for a drink with a person she hardly knew and heard was a womaniser.

I better go home and find something decent to wear for tonight, she thought. *Something not too revealing!*

It was then when she noticed the stocky body of Jack striding towards her, holding out his mobile phone. Daniela knew all too well the reason why. She welcomed him over and took the phone from him.

'Papá?'

'Hello, mija,' her father's voice said. 'Is everything okay?'

'Yes, why shouldn't it be?'

'I'm still a bit concerned about that incident from a couple of weeks ago. Maybe I should send an extra couple of hands to help Jose.'

'That won't be necessary,' Daniela smiled. 'He's bored as it is. There's only students and the elderly here. Not exactly a threat.'

'Right, well, if you need anything, just let me know, miljta.'

'Thanks, papá. I will.'

Then she thought for a moment and said, 'Papá?'

'Yes, mija?'

She stopped herself from asking the question she was thinking in her mind. Her father wouldn't hurt people she loved and cared for. Would he?

'It's nothing. I love you,' she said.

'Love you too,' came a hesitant reply. 'Put Jose back on.'

'Sure,' she said, handing the phone back to Jack. 'He wants you.'

Jack took the phone and walked back to his original position.

'I want to know her every move. The names of everyone she gets close to.'

'Si, Señor Flores,' replied Jack, staring towards Daniela, as she placed her books back into her bag.

6

IT was evening. Inspector Nicolas Kean just happened to be passing by Daniela's road. He rang the doorbell. She answered.

'Inspector, what good timing,' she said. 'I've given everyone the evening off, so it's just us!'

She had a silky white gown on and nothing else—her cleavage flawlessly exposed along with her pencil sharp nipples. Kean felt his legs tremble with excitement as he slowly headed up the stairs towards her—his heartbeat racing. Apart from a couple of lit candles, the place was dark.

'Red wine?' Daniela offered, pouring him a glass before he had a chance to answer.

'Why not? It's my night off,' he replied. Or was it? Indeed, if it was his night off, then what was he doing here?

The wine was smooth—easy to drink. In fact, so smooth that he consumed half of it quickly, as Daniela watched seductively. She slowly brushed her hand over the top of his thigh—making his heartbeat race even faster—he felt paralysed with excitement from her touch. The alcohol rushed to his brain. But he sensed something was wrong. His vision became impaired, and his head started to spin. He lost all strength, including his grip on the glass. It smashed into a thousand pieces on the ground, soaking his shoes with wine.

'What did you do?' he asked weakly.

Daniela let out a laugh so evil that it made his heart sink. Suddenly, he felt extreme nausea.

'The same thing that I did to Victor!' she said dryly. 'You just couldn't let this go could you, Inspector? Poking your nose in like a rat!'

He couldn't talk or move. He felt utterly paralysed. Sweat dribbled down his forehead and onto the bridge of his nose. He knew the end was close. What was worse was that he felt betrayed by the girl he loved …*loved? Where did that come from? I hardly know her! And if I did, I wouldn't be in this situation, with Rohypnol running through my veins,* he thought.

Jack walked into the room with a smug look on his face.

'Throw him into the water!' ordered Daniela. Then she stopped with a fazed look on her face when Kean's phone started ringing in his pocket.

'They will trace the call! They will track you down!' he hysterically managed to yell with anger.

Daniela and Jack just stood there, frozen, blankly staring at him. Screaming out loud, Kean sat up with confusion, looking around the room. They were gone. He found himself in his bedroom, which was dimly lit up by the early light of dawn. Sweating like a pig, he felt relieved to escape from the nightmare, thanks to the ringing of his phone. Disoriented, he managed to check the time before answering it. It was just after five in the morning. O'Leary's name flashed on the phone's screen.

'John, what is it?' he grunted.

'Morning, Inspector, you better come down to the river opposite the White Owl pub! A body has been found lying face down in the water!'

'You've got to be kidding,' was Kean's reaction.

Another death, this time close to the city centre, was a wake-up call. Forensics was fast to arrive at the scene to seal off the area. The body of a young man lay lifelessly by the river. His arms were stretched out, forming the shape of a crucifix, and his head was entirely inside the water. His blonde hair had turned a greenish colour, waving in the River Stour's fast-flowing current.

'Another drowning. We've identified him as Harry Barnes. A third-year occupational therapy student at the college,' explained O'Leary, rubbing his hands warm in the early morning chill.

'Anything the cameras picked up?' Kean asked.

'Well, this is the thing, Inspector. The camera outside the White Owl where he'd been drinking doesn't seem to be working. We suspect it was tampered with.'

'Brilliant,' Kean said sarcastically.

O'Leary had a disappointed look on his face. One that the Inspector had seen many times before.

'What is it?' he asked.

'He was having a drink with Daniela Flores,' O'Leary replied.

Kean froze and was too stunned to speak. His dream suddenly replayed in his mind. His conscience kept telling him Daniela was a serial killer—even though his heart told him otherwise.

'She's down at the station with Jose Perez,' added O'Leary.

Pamela, who was in charge of the forensic team, walked up to Kean.

'Inspector,' she said with a friendly smile as she removed her latex gloves.

'Morning,' Kean said. 'Any thoughts?'

She shook her head. 'Hopefully, a post-mortem should reveal some answers.'

'Can a check for Rohypnol be the first thing on the list?'

Pamela's facial expression changed at the odd request. 'So, you think it might be connected to the Victor Silva case?'

'I'm not ruling it out,' admitted Kean. 'But we need to look at all possibilities.'

'I'll get on it right away.'

'Thank you.'

Daniela looked worried as she walked into the interrogation room. She sat down opposite Kean, her face pale and her eyes swollen. O'Leary was already next door questioning Jack.

'Is there anything you want to say?' asked Kean, taking a deep breath.

Daniela shook her head and said, 'What do you want me to say? That I killed him?'

'Come on, Daniela! There are now two people dead! Both of whom you had close contact with!' Kean snapped. 'Even if I believe you, no one else will!'

'Listen! I agreed to have one quick drink with Harry! He stayed behind at the pub when I left.'

The Inspector's phone rang. Excusing himself, he immediately answered it when he saw the call was from Dr Gami.

'Inspector, the autopsy examination isn't complete yet, but I thought you might be interested to know that, again, a trace of Rohypnol *was* found in the body. And this time at a much higher quantity, indicating it was taken in the last twelve hours.'

'Incredible. Thank you, Doctor,' Kean said, hanging up with a deep sigh.

'There's no escaping from the fact that you and Jack are prime suspects,' he said to Daniela.

'Arrest us then, Inspector!' she replied, looking deep into his eyes. 'But I know we're both innocent, and that's enough for me. Just how would the police force look if they falsely arrested the Mexican Ambassador's daughter and her bodyguard?'

Kean knew that she had a good point. These two murder cases had to be treated with the utmost delicacy or it could turn political.

'I'm going to need to search your houses again,' he stuttered, feeling slightly hot under the collar.

She let out a short laugh. 'You're going around in circles. Haven't you already done that?'

This time a more intense search took place with more police to look deeper through the two maisonettes. Driven by the Inspector, Daniela sat at the back, thoughtfully looking out the window. Neither of them said a word. He hoped that he was mistaken about her being involved, but the voice in his head told him that it was too much of a coincidence. The similarities between the two deaths were uncanny— they both involved Rohypnol and death by drowning.

The two suspects waited in separate police cars while two different searches simultaneously took place. The result was the same, nothing relevant was found.

After the search units left, Kean stayed behind to ask Daniela a couple more questions.

'Please help me out here! Both the victims that you dated ended up dying the same way. How's that possible? Do you have any enemies that you know of? Maybe a jealous ex-boyfriend?' asked Kean as she hung her coat with shaky hands on the hanger next to the front door.

The maid had not yet returned after the place had been searched, and Jack was at his place downstairs, making sure that not too many things had been disturbed. Some people can get incredibly restless after having their homes searched, and Kean imagined that Jack was one of them.

'No jealous ex-boyfriends or enemies that I know of. Your guess is as good as mine,' answered Daniela, looking vulnerable.

'Listen, I believe you had nothing to do with it. But others won't see it that way.'

'I'm really scared,' she whispered with watery eyes.

Kean didn't realise at first how close together they were standing.

'I know,' he whispered back—as he felt the tip of his fingers touch hers.

He felt lost in her eyes. For a moment, it was as if they were the only two people living on the planet. No one else existed—or mattered. Not being able to hold back, they moved closer to one another, their bodies thrusting tightly together and their lips locking. After a kiss that lasted for a couple of seconds, Daniela pulled back.

'I'm sorry,' she said softly, gently brushing her hair to the side with her fingers.

'Don't be,' breathed Kean.

Both feeling awkward, they were quiet for a moment or two.

'Would you like a tea or coffee?' she said, breaking the ice.

Kean was just about to answer when he suddenly recalled the dream. Although he wanted to trust her, and his gut instinct told him that she was innocent, he declined the coffee. He was enchanted by her beauty, just like the two victims had been. With a sudden feeling of guilt, he excused himself and left. He should never have crossed the line. He had to somehow distance himself from Daniela.

On the way back to the station, X called.

'Well, Inspector, aren't we the naughty one?' his distorted voice teased. 'If you aren't careful, it could be you next going for a swim.'

Kean's heart skipped a beat.

'Don't worry. Your secret is safe with me,' mocked X.

'How did you know?' Kean asked, trying not to lose focus on the road ahead.

'I've been keeping a close eye on Miss Flores. And her bodyguard, Jack! I can assure you that they had nothing to do with the murder of Harry Barnes.'

'How can you be so sure?'

'Daniela left the pub early. Harry Barnes stayed on to have more drinks with some friends.'

'That's also what she said. Did you see who his friends were?'

'No, I didn't. The place was packed. I followed Daniela and her bodyguard, Jose, home.'

'I'll check the cameras.'

'Now that's another mystery,' sighed X. 'All the security cameras around the crime scene area were tampered with.'

7

SALEEM kept a low profile inside the studio flat on the outskirts of the city. It rained for three days non-stop in Birmingham. He couldn't wait to move south where it wasn't as cold and also rained less. Sitting on the floor in the corner of the room, nervously shaking his leg and tapping his heel on the ground, he waited impatiently.

His uncle, Usman, said that he would be there with the package shortly after 3pm. He worked on the estate, so it wouldn't take long for him to arrive. No doubt the police were sniffing around by now. But Saleem had had enough. There was no way he was going back to the asylum, or even worse—jail. He'd always been neglected by his parents, who were elderly. He'd dropped out of school at a young age—been in numerous gangs—made a living out of petty theft and then by selling drugs. But now, it was time for a change. Saleem Raza would exist no more, and a different person would be born—on the outside a better person—one who had received a public-school education and outstanding A-levels. Oh yes …a new identity too.

He'd be putting two fingers to the dysfunctional life he had here in Birmingham.

His next destination was Canterbury, where someone special would be waiting for him—although she didn't know it yet. Her name was *Daniela Flores*.

He first saw her in a magazine that covered the wedding of Maria Cruz, a Mexican actress. She had married James Henry, a billionaire entrepreneur. But it was Daniela, who was a guest at the wedding, who stole the show with her beauty in that silver dress she wore. After, Saleem religiously followed her social media accounts. He followed her every move. She was the daughter of the Mexican Ambassador to London—and a rare rose she was too—flawless and extravagant. She was single, and Saleem was going to make sure it stayed that way.

Suddenly, someone thumped hard on the door. Saleem forced himself off the ground and stumbled towards it.

'Yeah?' he called hesitantly.

'Come on, you little shit!' answered Uncle Usman's voice from the other side.

Saleem opened the door, and Usman rushed in.

'Easy!' sighed Saleem at his uncle's haste and aggression.

'This relaxed attitude will get you caught!' Usman warned him.

He sat on the old sofa, launching dust particles into the air. The place reeked of mould and stale spices. It was depressing. He had put it up for sale a while back, but no one showed any interest. He tried to rent it, but people ran a mile after viewing it. He knew Saleem would be safe here for the time being. If everything went to plan, this would probably be the last time he would see his troublesome nephew. He wasn't complaining about it as he would be happy to see the back of Saleem. There'd be no more cleaning up after his mess.

'So, did they give it to you?' implored Saleem.

'Yeah.'

Usman reached into his brown rucksack, and at first, he produced a passport and handed it over to Saleem.

'I hope you got rid of your original one,' he said.

Saleem nodded.

'Good.'

He examined the information inside, surprised to see that the passport photo was photoshopped. He now had a beard and was wearing glasses. He didn't even recognise himself.

'Specs?' he squeaked.

Usman took out a pair of glasses from the sack and handed them over.

'They are not prescription ones. Just plain old glass. I see you haven't shaved for a couple of days. Keep it that way.'

Saleem took the glasses and continued to examine the passport info. At least he was going to be two years younger. He looked at his new name and approved noddingly. It read Rashid Hassan Saadek.

'Here are your A-level documents for the university,' said Usman, handing over a stack of papers.

'And how about the other package?' Saleem asked.

Usman hesitated. 'I still don't know what you want it for.'

Saleem stopped and thought for a moment.

'They help me sleep at night. Insomnia is a bitch.'

'Fifty doses? I wasn't born yesterday, Sal.'

Usman scornfully looked at Saleem for a moment, who avoided eye contact. Eventually, he shook his head and sighed. Why did he care? He was getting rid of the spoilt brat forever. Plus, the way he saw it, he was doing his older sister a favour. Saleem impatiently snatched the package out of Usman's hand.

'Money well spent,' said Saleem to his uncle, who was still looking at him in disgust. 'And who said drugs are bad?'

'You never contact us again! This time I swear I will turn you in!' blasted Usman, slamming the door shut after Saleem had walked out.

8

THE unethical moment Kean had with Daniela kept replaying in his mind.

Well played, Nick! You just killed off the remainder of your career! A voice in his head told him.

Oh, shut up! If you had the chance, you know you'd do it again! Don't deny it!

The stress of crossing the line had hit him hard. Taking a pack of painkillers out of his desk drawer, he placed three pills on his tongue and gulped them down with a bottle of water. The room started to get darker as evening drew on. There was a soft knock on the door. He'd been working there for so long now that he'd memorised everyone's knocks.

'Come in, O'Leary.'

O'Leary walked in and nodded—not at all surprised that the Inspector guessed it was him. However, when he had guessed correctly a couple of years back, it was a surprise. Now, O'Leary just assumed that he was probably the only person who visited the Inspector's office—and it wouldn't be far from the truth.

'How can I help you, Serge?' asked Kean, opening a file labelled EVIDENCE.

'Inspector, I know that it isn't my call, but people are starting to talk,' O'Leary stuttered nervously.

'What do you mean?'

'There have been two murder cases closely linked with Daniela Flores, and she is still walking around freely…and so is her bodyguard.'

'You're right, O'Leary, it isn't your call. I believe Daniela Flores is innocent. And so is Perez.'

'If you say so, Inspector. But how can you be so sure?'

Kean felt himself twitching uncomfortably in his chair.

Answer that one, Nick! I'd like to see you try! The voice in his head mocked.

'Just a hunch. There's no solid evidence to indicate they were involved with the murders. In the meantime, I want all pharmacies in the Southeast region checked for any recent orders of Rohypnol! Keep a close eye on any dealers in the streets and clubs. I want to know if the drug has changed hands in the last couple of months!'

'Affirmative, Inspector.'

That evening Kean went home confused about his feelings for Daniela. Was she really a suspect—a possible serial killer? He wondered if he was in denial about who she really was. She seemed far too innocent to hurt anyone, but then that old saying came to his mind: the most innocent-looking people are often the ones who are guilty.

It felt unreal.

Her status is so high so why would she show any interest in someone like me in the first place? Asked the voice.

When he returned home that evening, he put on some comfortable clothes, chucked a ready-made steak and kidney pie into the microwave, and treated himself to a can of cold beer from the fridge. Switching on the news reminded him that, even at home, there was no escaping from work. Two familiar faces flashed on the TV screen. Ron and Julie, Victor's housemates, were being interviewed outside the house they shared with Victor and Rash.

'Such a shame! He was a nice person,' Julie played to the camera.

'It's frightening! There's definitely a local serial killer out on the loose!' Ron cut in.

The screen went back to the newsreader in the studio. Beneath him, the text on a dark blue stripe with a thick white font read: *Another Murder in South East Kent*.

'Both deaths seem identical to each other. A trace of Rohypnol, also known as the rape drug, was found in Harry Barnes's body—just like it was found in Victor Silva's two weeks ago. The East Kent Police department is working hard and urging anyone with any new information to come forward,' said the newsreader, forcing a stern look.

Replaying the day over and over in his head, Kean switched off the TV and headed to bed. He wondered if anyone would actually call in with new information after listening to the news. The two murders were nowhere near to being solved. In fact, the police had reached another dead end.

Lying in bed, he stared into the darkness. A strong urge to write to Daniela washed over him—it was a moment of weakness. He reached for his phone and sent a quick text without thinking.

I apologise for what happened at your place today, it said.

Straight after sending it, the reality of the situation struck him like a bolt of lightning, and he wished that he could unsend it—but it was too late.

The whole drama played out in his mind. The kiss would be exposed, rumours of an affair would start to circulate, and eventually, he'd have his badge confiscated. The bottom line was that he was playing with fire. But that didn't stop the way he felt about her.

Waiting half an hour in desperation for a reply to come through—he lost hope. Getting out of bed, he put his phone on charge and jumped into the shower—anything to bide time so he would be awake when she did reply. As the hot water rained down on his bare skin, all he could still think about was Daniela, and the magical moment they shared together. After a while in the shower—imagining her next to him with her naked body rubbing against his and making the most out of this electrifying pleasure—he eventually turned off the tap and jumped out. Drying as fast as he could—unsuccessfully—he rushed to the bedroom where his phone was charging.

This time there was a reply, which put a massive grin across his face, even though it was short and somewhat mysterious. It read: *Was very unexpected.*

9

ALBERTO Manuel Flores had spent a large portion of his life in North America, doing legal work for the Mexican Embassy in Washington DC. It was there that he was asked to keep an eye out for Veronica—a close family friend—who had come from Mexico to study. He was eight years her senior and he would regularly take her out for dinner and the occasional movie. She loved the newly found glamour of city life and adapted well to the metropolitan lifestyle. After dinner at a romantic restaurant one Friday evening, followed by a drunken night at a salsa bar, they had gotten close. One thing led to another, and the night ended up at his place. They'd become something of an item.

He'd sometimes stay at hers, and she'd sometimes stay over at his—though his apartment on Connecticut Avenue was more luxurious, so eventually, she had fully moved in. Oblivious to the truth, the family was relieved that he was there to keep an eye out for her.

It wasn't long before he proposed to her, and the most challenging thing they ever had to do was break the news to the family that they would marry. Some eyebrows were raised, but eventually, as time passed, everyone accepted that they were a family, and Veronica gave birth to a beautiful baby girl. They had named her Daniela.

When Daniela was seven, the family moved to Mexico City, and Alberto continued working for the Mexican government, mostly taking on asylum cases. Six years later, he was called for an urgent meeting at the embassy. An arrangement that would change the family's life forever—the Mexican Senate had ratified that the President of Mexico had sent an appointment favouring Alberto Flores to be the new Ambassador of Mexico to the United Kingdom. Although Veronica wasn't keen on the idea, Alberto couldn't refuse.

The family ended up moving to Central London. Daniela was sent to a boarding school and visited her parents at weekends. Even then, Alberto was too busy to see her most of the time. When she went to university, Alberto occasionally called Jose to get an update on Daniela's welfare. When he found out about her friends being killed, he increased the calls.

'Is there anything you want to share with me, mija?'

'No, papá, there isn't.'

'If you need any more security, just let me know,' he said to her over the phone while, again, she was in the library studying.

'Thanks, papá. I will,' her voice replied from the other end of the line—'Papá?'

'Yes, mijita?'

She was silent for a moment or two.

'It's nothing. I love you.'

He sighed and stopped scribbling on the large notepad in front of him on his desk. 'Love you too.'

Alberto hung up and looked at the man sitting opposite him. He wore a black suit which complemented his athletic figure. His waxed hair was combed back perfectly—making him appear incredibly confident and cool—with a strong jawline.

'Ricardo, your train ticket has been reserved, and your hotel is booked. There's something both Daniela and Jose aren't telling me. I want to know exactly what's going on. Make sure they don't notice you. And more importantly, find out who killed those young men!'

'Yes, Sir.'

'It could be political. If you suspect any foul play from the opposition, let me know!'

'I will.'

Alberto watched Ricardo leave. Questions were starting to be asked about the murders, and it wouldn't take long before the police would be sniffing around. He had warned Daniela to be careful many times. Any mishaps could spell the end of his ambassadorship.

That afternoon, two of Kean's colleagues based in London paid Mr. Flores a visit, asking permission to look at his bank statements. Although he thought it was an odd request, he complied. Not long after, Kean received a call from one of them telling him there was nothing suspect regarding any kind of drug trade. For the Inspector, it was undoubtedly a massive relief that the bank statements were clean. He certainly didn't want Daniela's family to be guilty—something that he kept quiet about. To the police force, it was another kick in the teeth. Again, the case had turned cold. The search for *The Silent Killer* continued—a name that had become popular among the media.

When Alberto went home that evening, he told Veronica everything.

'Another murder? Oh God!' she sighed in horror.

'A boy Daniela met up with for drinks. He was found dead, face down in the river the following morning,' breathed Alberto uncomfortably.

He watched his wife trying to shake off the shock.

'She told you that?'

'Course she didn't. Jose did,' replied Alberto, somewhat irritated by the question.

'So, two boys Daniela dated—dead,' stuttered Veronica, looking grim.

Alberto poured himself a scotch from the crystal vase with trembling hands.

'I blame you for her actions,' he said bluntly.

'My actions?'

'Yes. A young girl shouldn't be meeting men for drinks! As her mother, you should have taught her that.'

'Oh, that's rich coming from you!' Veronica snapped. 'And it is *exactly* what a young girl should be doing at university! Plus, they aren't men. They are only boys. Probably students, just like our Daniela.'

Alberto huffed with anger but managed to maintain his cool.

'Maybe if you weren't so strict with her before she went off to university, she wouldn't feel the urge to find her way in life! Boarding school was your idea after all!' Veronica added.

'That's not the point,' Alberto rasped. 'There's someone out there killing Daniela's friends. Who's to say she won't be next?'

'Don't you dare! And how dare you blame my mothering!' Veronica blasted, then started to sob uncontrollably.

'That's not all. The police have been treating Daniela as a suspect,' mumbled Alberto.

'What are we going to do?' sniffed Veronica looking pale with worry.

'I'm taking care of it,' he assured her.

10

THE Cuban Cocktail Bar was a favourite among students, especially on Friday and Saturday nights. Close to the city centre, it was the place to indulge in exotic cocktails and get away from the traditional pubs. It was the Inspector's third ever visit to the Cuban. The first was an eventless birthday night out with some of the boys. The second visit was work related. That night, he had witnessed something that he wished he could unsee. A young couple had come down from London for the weekend and stayed at the Marlow Hotel next to the Cuban. The Metropolitan police had sent a notification that they were dealers. The Inspector and his team had just missed them at the bar, so they raided their hotel room. Two men and two women, all in their early twenties, were involved in some kind of weird foursome. Everyone was naked. One of the women was lying on her back in bed, covered with lines of cocaine all over her body, as the others snorted it, while engaging in sexual activity at the same time. They didn't seem too

bothered when the police broke down the door—
especially the girl lying on the bed.

'*I love men in uniform,*' Kean remembered her saying in a posh accent.

The messages between Daniela and the Inspector had got more frequent and bordered on flirtatious. On Saturday, she mentioned that she would meet a few girls from her political science class for drinks down at the Cuban. Reading between the lines, Kean replied that she might bump into him there.

Way to go, Nick! You deserve to be jobless, mocked the voice inside his head.

Nicolas Kean looked at himself in the mirror with reassurance and answered back, 'It's okay. You're only doing your job.'

As usual, the place was packed like a can of sardines and reeked of sweat and stale perfume, with people talking loudly, trying to be heard over the loud Latin techno music blasting from the large speakers in the corners of the room. It would take a while to find Daniela in the crowd. Kean forced his way towards the bar at the far end, trying to keep an eye out for her at the same time.

It took at least ten minutes to order a mojito, and after another ten minutes, he felt someone tap on his shoulder. He turned and saw Daniela looking up and smiling.

'Hey,' she said with a slight blush. *Or it could be from the red lighting,* he thought.

'Hi!' Kean answered back, looking happy to see her.

He held out his hand, she did the same, and their hands locked tightly as they moved closer to each other. She smiled, looked deep into his eyes and held his gaze.

'Your hand is cold,' she said into his ear, so he could hear her over the loud music.

'It's because of the mojito,' he answered. 'Would you like one?'

Hesitating for a moment. 'Sure,' she replied.

He tried to get the attention of the barmen, but they all turned a blind eye. Suddenly, one of them smiled and walked over, and then the other rushed to take his order.

Just like buses, he thought to himself. *You wait all day, and suddenly two turn up.*

But he was mistaken. Daniela had waved them over. It was her they were rushing towards, not him. The Inspector almost laughed at how ridiculous they looked as they climbed over each other to take Daniela's order.

When she eventually got her mojito, he asked where her friends were. She told him that they were at the other side, near the pool tables.

'And how about Frankenstein's monster?'

She tried hard not to spray her drink at Kean with laughter.

'Jack's somewhere near where the girls are standing. Luckily, he can't follow me into the ladies,' she said. 'So,

Inspector Nicolas Kean, now it's your turn to be interrogated!'

'Oh God!' he laughed.

'Did you always live here in Canterbury?'

'I've been residing here for the last eight years,' he said, putting on a posh accent and making her giggle.

'Where were you before?'

'Ok, I'm going to start from the beginning—'

'A good place to start.'

'I was born and schooled in North London—then graduated in Canterbury with a triple first in sociology, psychology, and politics—'

'Not just a pretty face!'

'Then later, I attended Sidcup College for police training …before finding myself based back here in Canterbury.'

'Nice,' she said, taking a sip of mojito.

They chatted for about twenty minutes, this time more about her past, and when they finished their drinks, he asked her if they should go outside for some fresh air.

'I wouldn't mind a nice walk by the river,' she said. 'Quick! Before Frankenstein catches on!'

They made their way through the stubborn crowd of people—mostly students—too selfish to move out of the way. She turned and reached for his hand, making it easier to go through when people saw that they were together. Eventually, they reached the door. Kean could have sworn that someone was watching, and he was right. On the other side of the room, following them with his gaze like a gliding hawk from a distance, was Rash. Kean was startled to see him. Rash didn't twitch. Kean nodded slightly at him, and Rash raised a half-hearted smile.

'What is it?' asked Daniela when they were out the door.

'It was Rash. One of Victor's housemates.'

'Rash? Are you sure?'

'Yes, he was watching us. Probably shocked that we were holding hands.'

'That's unusual. He never used to go out. Certainly not to a place like this. He doesn't drink …or even socialise with anyone.'

'How well do you know him?'

'Actually, I knew him before meeting Victor. Coincidentally, he moved into the same house a couple of days after we started dating.'

'That is a coincidence,' Kean said, looking puzzled.

'Canterbury is a small place.'

'That is true.'

Passing the Marlow Theatre, they walked towards Westgate, where the River Stour ran through. There had always been a Bohemian feel about the Canterbury High Street, with its remarkable picturesque Cathedral and medieval-style buildings. Kean remembered his first visit there—looking around the city when he picked the university as his first choice. That's when he knew deep down it was his only option—a place with a peaceful aura and friendly faces.

They reached the river, locked hands, and slowly strolled towards the park, following the gently flowing water into the darkness. Kean moved closer to Daniela—letting go of her hand, and instead, gently wrapping his arm around her shoulder—allowing her head to rest on his chest. In return, she cupped her arm over his waist with a tight squeeze as they walked further along. Coming to a stop at the wooden bridge, they turned and faced each other. The condensation from her breath became fast with excitement. The park was still and silent—screams of drunken laughter and Irish folk music blasted from one of the pubs nearby. They kissed. This time it lasted longer as their bodies embraced, thrusting tightly against each other—almost keeping up with the rhythm of *Dirty Old Town*.

'My house is a ten-minute walk from here,' whispered Kean, trying to catch his breath. 'If you're feeling cold.'

She looked up and smiled at him.

They eventually arrived at his, hardly able to take their hands off each other. He felt drawn to her like a moth to a flame. Kean had never felt anything like it before. They found themselves in his bedroom.

'Have you got protection?' she breathed into his ear.

Kean nodded. The bedroom was dark—only dimly illuminated by the light in the corridor. He opened the top drawer next to the untidy bed, digging out a sachet from the Durex box.

They both got undressed, and she laid on her back while he nervously applied the protection. Once he had succeeded, he steadily crawled towards her, kissing her soft lips, and their naked bodies made contact. Like a spider, she wrapped her long legs around his body while he playfully forced himself inside her warmth. He felt on top of the world, doing his best to last as long as the excitement allowed him. She shivered with pleasure—burning his skin by scratching her long nails along his back and down to his buttocks. It was breath-taking—the excitement and the pain, then there came the big bang—the finale.

'You stallion,' she groaned, holding him even tighter.

They stayed joined together for a while after—maybe ten minutes—maybe more.

Eventually, she broke away, looked at the time, and told him that she had to go.

'Stay the night,' he offered, trying not to sound too needy.

'I don't think that's a good idea,' she said, slipping her silk panties back on.

After thinking about it for a moment, he agreed.

'No, you're right.'

She walked up to him and ran her fingers through his hair and down towards his muscular shoulder.

'Barbaro,' she breathed.

'What's that?' he smiled.

'Means attractive strong man,' she said, blushing.

'Well, don't know about that,' he modestly said with a grin.

Her phone kept vibrating in her bag. She ignored it at first.

'Probably Jack, wondering where the hell I am,' she grinned.

Eventually, taking her phone out, she looked confused when she saw Viola, the maid, calling. Viola never called. It was always Jack chasing after her, so why was Viola calling?

When Daniela answered, her expression changed from worried to anxious. Jack was missing, and he wasn't answering his phone.

'He's not with me,' Daniela told Viola, somewhat ashamed that she was not with Jack. 'Okay, I'll try calling him too.'

She hung up and worriedly looked up at Kean.

'Maybe he's still in the bar and can't hear his phone,' he said.

She checked the time on her phone and shook her head. 'Impossible. He uses an earpiece. Always answers. He would have left that place long ago when he noticed I didn't return from the bathroom.'

'Is this the first time you left his sight?'

'He lost track of me a couple of times before but managed to locate me straight away. He'd definitely answer Viola's call in case I'd returned home without him.'

'Come on!' Kean said, jumping out of bed and hurriedly putting on his clothes. 'I'll go search for Jack after dropping you home.'

'I'll come to look with you,' she said.

'No, best I go alone.'

Opening the front door, the Inspector allowed Daniela to exit before him as a chilly wind rushed into the corridor. They paced towards his blue Ford Fiesta and he pressed on the key, unlocking its doors—but Daniela stopped cold and glared at the car.

'Being royalty, probably not the type of ride you're used to, but this is all I have on offer—' chuckled Kean.

'What's that?' Daniela asked, signalling at the car's exhaust.

'What the—'

Kean focused hard—there was something slightly reflecting the streetlight. It appeared pointy, sharp, and fierce. Directing his phone's torchlight towards it, he saw a face of a crow poking out the exhaust pipe.

'Fuck's sake!' he breathed in bewilderment.

'Is it dead?' Daniela asked, looking nauseous.

'Doesn't appear to be struggling or making any noise, so I guess so.'

Getting a pair of latex gloves from the car, he pulled the lifeless bird out, baffled at how it got squeezed in there.

'Wonder if a cat did it.'

'Shouldn't think so,' said Kean, placing the dead bird into a plastic bag. 'Someone tried to kill us from carbon monoxide poisoning!'

Daniela's eyes widened.

'What!? Are you sure?'

'If it was killed by a cat, there would be blood or a bite wound. Plus, a cat wouldn't be able to shove a bird up an exhaust pipe. This was intentional. It needs to go to the lab for examination. Maybe they can find some kind of clue on how it was killed.'

11

JULIE West had a tragic and lonely childhood. Unlike most of her cousins, she had no siblings, and when growing up this used to sadden her. But that was nothing compared to what was to come. She was nine when, on a rainy Saturday, her father planned to treat her to a film at the cinema. She didn't really care about the film. It was all about the popcorn. She loved the popcorn—the sweet smell of it when entering the cinema made her happy—and on the way, she thought about what drink she would have. Coke—or lemonade?

But little did Julie and her father know that this would be their final trip together to the cinema—or anywhere, as a matter of fact. The speeding car came out of nowhere, materialised in front of them, and was going in the wrong direction on the one-way system—both vehicles skidded uncontrollably, loudly screeching their breaks along the wet road. The last thing Julie could remember was the terrified eyes of the elderly lady behind the wheel. The result—a head-on collision and only one survivor. Julie suffered a life-threatening head injury, had one major surgery and spent two months in ICU in critical condition before being discharged to a ward.

It was all downhill from there. Her uncle, John, broke the sad news about her father. Something had triggered Julie's appetite. She found comfort in eating. She ate and ate—the sweets, the chocolate …the popcorn—yes, the popcorn, she couldn't get enough of it. Within a year, she had put on so much weight that she had become obese.

Her mother was a nervous wreck—unable to look after Julie. Therefore, for a while, Julie stayed with her Uncle John, a barrister who ran a successful law firm in central London. Because of his busy schedule, he hardly had any time for Julie. She was looked after by a nanny, who smoked more than babysat.

'Take a seat,' Uncle John said to her when he came home late one evening after the nanny left.

Julie did, and he sat opposite her with a somewhat sympathetic look.

'What is it?' she asked. 'Why do you always look at me like you're feeling sorry for me?'

'I don't feel sorry for you,' he lied—But what he was really thinking was, was *'Yes, with your father dead and your mother being in a suicidal state, I have never felt so sorry for anyone in the world.'*

She shrugged and rolled her eyes.

'As you are aware, mummy is not well. She needs to be admitted to a special clinic. You need to start school again soon.'

'Great. I miss my friends. But—I don't want them to see me like this,' she said, shamefully gesturing at her obese body.

'Yes, you do need to start eating less, darling. But the main reason I wanted to talk to you is that I can't always be there for you as I'm incredibly busy. However, I will do everything I can to make sure you get a good education. I've also spoken to your mummy, and she agreed that you should go to boarding school.'

'Boarding school? But I am only nine,' Julie said, as her face fell. She didn't know much about boarding schools, but she had heard they were scary places—and the ones she saw in movies were pretty bad too—not much different to orphanages, she imagined.

Although she didn't like the idea, she *was* only nine and had no choice. It was hell for an overweight nine-year-old girl who had just lost her father and the mother she used to know. She was not only bullied by the other students, but by the teachers too. Seven years later, when she was sixteen, she got caught smoking cannabis and was expelled.

With her uncle keeping her at arm's length and her mother locked away in a mental asylum, Julie—now a chain smoker and unrecognisably thin—worked as a waitress at a sandwich bar in South London. She smoked more than she ate, which in hindsight helped her lose all the weight she'd put on—and the rest.

It was a dull day when a young man came in to order a cheese special with extra pickle. He and Julie got talking. His name was Ron Blates and he was going to start a teaching degree at the University of Bristol after the summer holidays. By the end of the holidays, Julie and Ron had got close. She developed a sudden obsession about moving to Canterbury. Ron was so mad about Julie that he managed get a transfer to the university in Canterbury. He didn't realise something was not quite right about her. As far as he was concerned, she could do no wrong.

Julie waited for everyone to leave the house the morning Inspector Nicolas Kean searched Victor's room. She was just about to go upstairs when Ron left, but within two minutes, he was back.

'Did you use my car this week?' he asked her, looking puzzled.

Julie swallowed hard. 'No, why would I?' she squeaked.

'The petrol level has gone down, and I'm sure I parked it closer to the house when I got back from London on Sunday.'

'With Victor's death and the police sniffing around—it has all been mentally exhausting for all of us!' Julie explained.

Ron, still confused by the car, thought for a moment before replying, 'Yeah, I suppose.'

After kissing Ron goodbye, Julie finally managed to go upstairs. From her jeans pocket, she produced a master key and opened Rash's bedroom door. Once inside, she knew exactly where to look. There was a slight creaking sound from the stairs. She rushed out and looked down the staircase, but no one was there.

With a nervous sigh, she went back into Rash's bedroom and opened the cupboard. Sliding the hangers with Rash's clothes on to one side, she reached in and took out a box from the back of the closet. Removing the lid, she peeked inside, just as stunned as the first time she had seen the large number of green pills resting in their packages.

Then something else resting beneath the box caught her eye—something she hadn't noticed before. She reached back into the cupboard and picked it up. It was a notebook. Curiously, she opened it. Secretly taken photos of Daniela and cut-outs from magazines and newspapers were glued to almost every page—even if she was only in the background of most of the photos. But that wasn't all. There were pages with writing showing Daniela's schedule, where she went, and the times of all her lectures. On one of the pages, a large heart was sketched with an arrow through it. Inside the heart were the letters D and R—Yep, Rash was an actual stalker who was obsessed with Daniela.

Julie smiled to herself as she carefully placed the box and the notebook back into the cupboard.

<h1 style="text-align:center">12</h1>

KEAN dropped the sealed bag with the dead crow to the police station and then notified Pamela so she could take it in for examination. On the way to Daniela's house, O'Leary alerted all the on-duty police to keep an eye out for Jack, while the Inspector went straight to the Cuban to review the CCTV footage. The first person he recognised was Rash, who walked straight out after he and Daniela had left. Jack loitered around the ladies' toilets for a while, waiting for Daniela to come out, but she never did. When he was sure they were empty, he disappeared into the ladies, and a couple of seconds later, stormed back out in sheer panic, ploughing through the herds of people and out the front door. That was the last time Jack was seen that night.

After searching until three in the morning and then filing a missing person's report at the station, Kean went home frustrated. The following morning when he was woken by an early call from O'Leary, he could hardly open his eyes.

Yeah?' he grunted, answering the call.

'Inspector, Jose Perez has been found,' O'Leary said coldly.

'What!? Where was he?' Kean asked, sleepily rubbing his eyes with a yawn.

'Dangling off a bush, by the city wall …dead.'

Kean stopped for a moment to register what O'Leary had just told him.

'Forensics is investigating now. According to a witness, he was pushed off the path at the top of the wall—by what appeared to be a jogger,' added O'Leary.

'Un-bloody-believable!' exclaimed Kean. 'Meet me there. I'll be about fifteen minutes.'

'I'm already here, Inspector.'

The stone city walls in Canterbury were originally built by the Romans and are six metres tall, so the bush Jack fell into seemed just as damaged as he was. Apart from his feet, his entire body was camouflaged by the leaves, which explained why he wasn't found during the night. The place was swarming with reporters. Kean had a microphone shoved into his face the moment he arrived.

'Inspector, is this related to the other murders?' asked a reporter, trying to keep up with him.

'We don't even know if it is a murder,' he said, not breaking his stride.

'How about a suicide?' asked the reporter, trying to catch his breath.

'We're not ruling anything out.' Kean called back at him, hurrying towards O'Leary.

'Where's the witness, Serge?'

O'Leary pointed at a lady with scruffy blonde hair and a pale face standing close by. As Kean walked up to her, a strong smell of stale alcohol burnt his nostrils.

'Hello, I'm Inspector Kean. Can you tell me exactly what you saw last night?'

'You what?'

'What did you see last night, madam?' repeated Kean, keeping a fair distance from her.

'I already said what I saw,' she slurred. 'You police are all messed up!'

Great! The only witness is a tramp! At least it's better than no witness—actually, I'm not so sure. Thought Kean.

'Can you tell me again in more detail?' he asked her.

She tried to focus her befuddled eyes on him and frowned.

'Well,' she started off. 'This giant of a man was walkin, you see. And was stopped by a jogger who said somethin to 'em. He then went lookin' over that edge over there—and the jogger pushed the poor bastard over! It happened very quickly.'

'Can you describe what the jogger looked like?'

'It was dark. But a short, skinny fella he was. Had one of them baseball caps.'

The Inspector thanked the lady and headed over to the small crowd surrounding Jack's body dangling lifelessly from the bush. The area was taped to keep the reporters and the pedestrians—who were marvelling at the scene—from getting too close.

When O'Leary saw Kean, he puffed his cheeks, shook his head and said. 'I already asked forensics to do a drugs test.'

'Very wise,' replied Kean. 'Based on what the witness said, I doubt that there will be any though.'

'So, you think this isn't connected to the other two cases?'

'I think there's a connection. But if it is the same person, then this wasn't planned like the other two incidents. It all seems a bit *improvised*.'

O'Leary scratched his head. 'Do you think we should question Daniela Flores again, Inspector? Do you think she had something to do with this?' he asked softly. 'After all, it is her bodyguard.'

'No, she didn't.'

'But how can you be so sure?'

Kean hesitated and answered. 'Because she was with me.'

There was another short pause.

'I see,' said O'Leary, looking puzzled. He was about to say something else but caught himself.

Pamela walked up to them. She looked sharp for this time of the morning with her shiny black hair tied in a perfect ponytail and spectacles that gave her an authoritative look. In one hand, she steadily carried a metal case which Kean assumed contained some samples.

'Where'd you find the dead crow?' she asked, carefully placing the case on the ground.

'Stuffed up my car's exhaust pipe. So, did you find anything?' asked Kean, trying not to sound too impatient.

'As a matter of fact, yes—Rohypnol.'

Coffee in hand, X watched the circus of police and reporters from a distance, wishing that he had followed Jack instead of Daniela to the Inspector's house the night before. He was now sure that there were two killers. Last night when he was hiding in the dark, he had seen the distinct shape of one of them. He was getting ready to call Kean about the dead bird. But Daniela had already noticed it in the exhaust pipe.

As he watched Inspector Kean talking to Pamela and O'Leary, he called Kean with the voice changer app. Kean swiftly moved away before he answered.

'Inspector, the number of deaths is rising. There is more than one person involved.'

'How did you come to that conclusion?' Kean asked curiously.

'While you were having your fun with Miss Flores, a large man with a beard and glasses in a thick anorak was wandering around your car, carrying a dead crow. Word has it that the person who pushed Jack over the edge was petite and sporting a tracksuit,' explained X.

Standing not so far away from X, watching the drama like a tiger from a distance, was Ricardo. He was also on the phone giving updates to the Ambassador.

'Find out who's responsible for this and keep a close eye on Daniela until the transport from London arrives,' said Alberto, his voice shaky.

'Yes, sir,'

When Ricardo hung up, he looked up and saw a man staring towards him with a slight smile. He had a takeaway coffee in his hand in one of those carton cups and wore a white anorak, black cap, and sunglasses. X could smell a spy from a mile away. And Ricardo stood out like a sore thumb. He quickly moved away. When he looked back, X was gone.

13

'NO, I won't come back!' Daniela shouted at Alberto with frustration as her father huffed at the other end of the line, trying to stay calm. Although hot-blooded, he was always calm when it came to his daughter—who was still in tears and shocked about Jack's death.

'Mijita, for all we know, your life might be in great danger. And I cannot take any risks. A car will be sent for you right away. Make sure you're packed and ready to go. Until the killer is caught, you will stay under protection—in London!'

'But how about my lectures? I can't miss my lectures. I have exams coming up!'

'You'll have to give the lectures a miss for now.'

'All my life you've controlled me. For once, let me have my freedom, Papá.'

There was a moment's silence as Alberto thought hard. He was stuck between his wife's and his daughter's wishes, not for the first time—and he was sure it wouldn't be the last.

'If something were to happen to you, I would never forgive myself. So please come home,' he begged her. This was the first time Daniela saw an almost human side to her father. Somewhere under the ice was a warm heart, no doubt.

'You're very stubborn, just like me,' he admitted, and Daniela felt a slight smile at the other end of the line. When she was a toddler, he had first sensed a glimmer of his characteristics in her—although she had her mother's beauty.

'Can't you just send more security, instead?'

'The police have already been here. There's a huge investigation going on. Once the media finds out who Jose is, the paparazzi will shadow you everywhere. You haven't got a choice, mijita. You're coming to London!'

'Fine! I'll come! But don't expect me to stay long!' Daniela blared.

'Good. Make sure you're ready. Don't keep the driver waiting. And mija—someone is already guarding the house.'

'Who? I can't see anyone?' Daniela asked, peeking out the window, scanning every inch of the private road.

'Oh, he's there alright,' Alberto said.

Kean was faced with a mountain of paperwork that was to be added to the growing murder case file of *The Silent Killer*. Although Jack's case didn't have the other murders' characteristics—they certainly all had one thing in common: All the victims were close to Daniela. The Inspector received a call from Superintendent Michael Lowe, who immediately asked to see him in his office. Placing the files on the side of his desk, he headed for the Superintendent's office.

He knocked firmly on the door, and Lowe invited him in. It had always surprised Kean that the Superintendent's office was the same size as his, if not slightly smaller. The room was cluttered with files and behind the desk was a pin-board with postcards and holiday snaps.

'Sit down,' Lowe commanded.

Kean placed himself on the seat and locked eyes with the Superintendent, who seemed to have a permanent frown. Whenever he visited, he was usually greeted with a friendly smile, but not today, and he knew the reason. His relationship with Daniela hadn't exactly been kept a secret. He had kicked himself many times—promising himself he would steer clear from her. But the feelings were so strong that his personal ethics and professional morals had all but evaporated.

'Inspector, you've been on the force for eight years now. And I have watched you climb up the ranks. You've become a valuable member of the team throughout the years. But now, I regret to hear you've been crossing the line with a suspect. I called you here to hear your side of the story.'

'She is not a suspect, Superintendent. And we now know that there are two people involved, and none of them are Daniela,' explained Kean as calmly as his nerves allowed him to.

'Who are they? I need more evidence!'

'One is a large man with a beard, who possibly wears glasses. He placed a dead crow into the exhaust pipe of my car, and the other is a—'

Kean froze as X's voice suddenly echoed in his ears '...*a large figure with a beard and glasses*!'

Then the image of Rash watching him and Daniela at the Cuban played in his mind.

'Superintendent! I think I know who he might be!' he stuttered.

Lowe looked confused. 'Who?'

'One of Victor's housemates! His name is Rash!'

'Victor?'

'Yes, Victor Silva. The first victim.'

'Great, in that case, pass this information to Inspector Noel.'

'Inspector Noel?'

'The disciplinary board will start investigating your relationship with Daniela Flores. From now on I think it's best if Noel is in charge of the case.'

Kean was too stunned to speak. Noel was in no way the right person for this case. He would go the extra mile to prove Daniela guilty, even though she wasn't. He suddenly felt sick to his stomach. His phone vibrated in his blazer's inner pocket. Taking it out, he saw it was O'Leary calling and hesitated.

'Answer it,' said Lowe.

Kean did. 'Yes, Sergeant O'Leary!'

'Inspector, three boxes of Rohypnol have just been located!'

'Where!?' Kean asked, springing up in excitement.

'26 East Gate Drive.'

'Isn't that where Victor Silva lived?'

'Affirmative.'

'I'll call you back,' said Kean, hanging up and holding Lowe's gaze.

The Superintendent shook his head dismissively. 'Just go,' he grunted. 'You can update Noel after he returns from Ashford.'

'Will that be necessary?' asked Kean. 'Looks like we found who it is!'

'You know, from all my years of policing, there's one thing that I have learned,' said Lowe.

'What's that?'

'It's never over until the court says it is.'

Before walking out the door, Kean paused and took a moment to think about it.

When Kean and O'Leary arrived at 26 East Gate Drive's front door, they were greeted by Julie and Ron. Like last time, the place was stuffy and dark. Obviously, none of the tenants were enthusiastic about cleaning.

Julie seemed overly excited and it appeared to Kean that she was being overdramatic. Ron was silent and looked worried. The two policemen followed them up the stairs and into Rash's room, which was the first on the right side, straight after the stairs.

'He ain't been home for a couple of days. Ron went into his room lookin' for a pen, and that's where he found the pills,' explained Julie hysterically.

'Yes, that's right, suddenly all my pens went missing, so Julie said that Rash had loads lying around.'

Compared to the rest of the house, this room was neat and tidy and appeared larger than Victor's. On the desk at the left, opposite the bed (which was neatly made), were three random packets labelled Rohypnol. One of them was open, with the silver inside pulled out halfway, exposing at least eight pills missing from the packet. The Inspector's heart jumped. There was a folded piece of paper and a notebook next to the Rohypnol boxes.

'Did anyone touch or move anything around?' asked O'Leary as he started taking photos of the items on the desk with his phone.

'Yeah, I picked up one of the boxes,' said Ron, worriedly.

'Nothing else in here should be touched,' explained O'Leary, taking a close-up photo of one of the green pills.

'Where's Rash?' asked Kean, putting on a pair of latex gloves so that he could handle the packets.

'Haven't seen him for a couple of days,' answered Julie.

Kean picked the paper up and unfolded it. A note typed on the computer read: *I cannot take it anymore. Love you forever Daniela.* Kean then looked inside the notebook and what he saw made his hands tremble with anxiety as sweat slid down his forehead. Rash had to be found—and fast!

After the two policemen left, Ron turned to Julie and shot her a look of suspicion.

'What you staring at?' she grunted.

'You've been acting different for some time.'

'No, I haven't.'

'Yeah—you have. Ever since Victor disappeared. With no telling the police and watching your back.'

'Shut up, you paranoid prick!'

'You know something, don't you!' Ron pushed. She tried to get past him but he held her wrists.

'Let go of me!' she snapped, breaking free.

He let out a deep sigh as he watched her disappear down the stairs. Suddenly, a feeling of anxiety washed over him. He had to get out of this relationship, and fast.

14

THE two inspectors (Kean and Noel) and four sergeants (O'Leary, Felling, Rickson and Reynolds) gathered in the room 6 meeting room on the third floor of the police station. Noel stood next to Kean, trying to look important, while the others sat listening to Kean.

'So, we now have a culprit …but he's missing. Twenty-one Rohypnol pills—a diary stating his obsession for Miss Daniela Flores …and a note saying that he couldn't take it any longer and admitting his love for Daniela, have been recovered from his bedroom,' explained Kean, as he went through a slideshow showing photos of the evidence.

'Now that we know who he is, we'll find him in no time!' interrupted Noel. The others ignored him and continued to focus on Kean.

'So, the million-dollar question …is this really a suicide note?' he asked the group.

Sergeant Lawrence Felling raised his hand and answered, 'Maybe he knew that he couldn't have her, and so he decided the only way out was to take his own life?'

'Evidently, but if so, then where's the body? There's something we're missing, along with the nine Rohypnol tablets. Something's not quite right.'

'Maybe he didn't commit suicide at all. Maybe he wants to make us believe that he did. For all we know, he might be getting ready to kill again,' said Rickson, sending shivers down Kean's spine, knowing that he could be the next target.

'Then why would he leave the notebook and the pills out in the open on his desk?' asked Sergeant Claire Reynolds, who was also newly assigned to the case.

'Sounds like a definite suicide to me. At least there'll be no more danger in the streets,' stated Noel smugly.

'What about the jogger who pushed Jose Alves to his death?' asked Kean.

'What about him? It was Rash all along!'

'It doesn't fit Rash's description.'

'According to a short-sighted tramp-lady!' sniffed Noel.

'Still, we can't dismiss that. Is there anything you'd like to add Inspector Griffith,' said Kean, watching the disappointed faces of the sergeants.

Proudly stepping forward, chest first, Noel made eye contact with each sergeant, raising a slight smile. 'We can safely say that Rashid Hassan Saadek is a sociopath who is blatantly obsessed with Daniela Flores. Therefore, he decided to get rid of anyone who got close to her.'

'So, what's the next step?' asked O'Leary.

'Whether he's alive or dead, we need to find him,' answered Noel.

'Actually, a background search on Rash would be wise,' Kean interrupted.

'Yes …a background search, Sergeant Reynolds?' said Noel.

'Will do, Inspector,' answered Reynolds, taking notes.

After the briefing, on the way home, Kean knew he couldn't let the case go, even though he'd been relieved. He needed to make sure Daniela was safe. He was sure Rash wasn't the only person involved. One question kept running through his mind: *Who was the night jogger?*

Alberto anxiously waited in his study, staring out of the large window behind his desk as he took a sip of scotch, welcoming the fine malt that burned his throat as it worked its way down. It was another grey day in London—dark clouds were threatening to erupt at any second, with hail and thunder in the forecast. Not a perfect day to be on the road. The car had left for Canterbury a while ago and was due to arrive there in just over two hours—traffic permitting. On an ordinary day with no traffic or roadworks, the journey would usually take an hour and a half.

His mobile rang loudly, vibrating along his desk. He answered right away when he saw it was Daniela calling.

'Papá' said her voice at the other end. 'The killer has been identified!'

She sounded drained like all the energy had been sucked out of her.

'Really? Who was it?'

'One of the students. His name is Rash. He was Victor's housemate.'

'Victor? Oh, your friend who was murdered.'

'Si, Papá, they reckon Rash killed himself, but they haven't found him yet. He left a suicide note.'

'Interesting. So, his body hasn't been found?'

'Not yet, but the police are searching for it. At least I'm safe now and don't have to come to London.'

'Actually, mija, you do, until they are certain that he is actually dead or has been caught. The car should be there to pick you up in a couple of hours.'

'But Papá—'

'No buts!'

Daniela was too tired to argue so she gave in.

'Si Papa,' she answered softly.

When Alberto hung up, the buzzer on his office phone went. *Probably more documents to be signed or another meeting to be arranged,* he thought to himself. Being ambassador certainly wasn't as glamorous as people had imagined. A lot of the days were mundane.

When he answered, his secretary told him that his brother had come.

'Juan? Send him through, Valeria.'

Juan was six years his younger. He lived in Mexico City and had only recently finished a fifteen-year sentence for major fraud. He had typically spent most of his time drinking while thinking of different ways of making quick money. But since coming out of jail, it seemed the fasted way was to ask Alberto.

'Hello, brother!' he said as he walked into Alberto's office.

Alberto Flores walked up to his younger sibling and gave him a hug.

'When did you get here?'

'Last night. Wanted to surprise you!'

'Well, you certainly did. Take a seat,' said Alberto, returning to his desk. 'So, is this why you wanted to borrow a thousand bucks last week? For flight tickets.'

'You got me! I really appreciate your help, brother. But hopefully, it won't be for much longer. I've got something lined up.'

Alberto shot Juan a look and held his gaze. 'Is it legal?'

'Yes, of course,' Juan laughed.

'Good. So, it will be a fresh start.'

'I'll tell you about it later. Now I'll enjoy a nice whisky. What's wrong? You don't look happy.'

'It's been one hell of a week.'

'I suppose being ambassador brings huge responsibilities. How is everyone? Veronica? Daniela?' asked Juan with a forced grin.

'Not great. Daniela might be in danger. Jose was killed last night.'

'That's terrible! Sorry to hear …I had no idea. Do we know who's behind it?'

'Apparently, they tracked someone down who appears to be obsessed with Daniela, but he's disappeared. The police suspect that he killed a couple of her friends—and now Jose.'

Juan shook his head in dismay. 'To think Jose was killed in Canterbury when he survived a war in Mexico is beyond belief!'

'Right.'

'So, what are you going to do about it?'

'Daniela is coming home. She'll be safe here.'

Juan stood up and walked over to Alberto, who nervously sat on his chair, and placed a hand on his brother's slumped shoulder.

'If there's anything I can do, let me know,' he said with a sympathetic smile.

Alberto gave his hand a friendly pat. 'Thank you, brother. I'll take care of it myself.'

15

OPENING a cold can of beer, Kean got stuck into The Witness's Secret by Tom J Rane, a novel that he'd been neglecting for some time. He needed something to take his mind off the case and refresh, but there was no use trying. Obviously, Rash was involved, but he didn't fit the description of the night jogger. Inspector Noel Griffiths would claim victory if Rash was found dead—and probably an even greater victory if he was found alive— and someone would get away with murder.

Kean was just about to call X to see if he had any new information when the doorbell rang.

He opened the door, surprised to see Daniela standing there. She was wearing a leather jacket matching her leather boots and jeans with black rose patterns knitted on. She had such a perfect physique that even if she was clothed in rags, Kean was sure she'd still look amazing.

'Daniela, I wasn't expecting to see you!' he gasped.

'I came to say goodbye. I'm going to London. I don't know how long for.'

Kean hesitated for a moment.

'Maybe that's the best thing,' is all he could think to say; although he wanted to say a lot more, he was caught off guard.

'Yes, maybe it is.'

'I've been removed from the case.'

'Why?'

'Daniela, listen, they know about us. We really shouldn't see each other—but I can't stop myself.'

There was a long pause.

'I'm sorry you've been taken off the case …it's all my fault,' she replied.

'Not your fault at all,' he said, then gestured for her to follow him to the lounge where he'd been reading. 'I should've known better. But I have no regrets. Please, take a seat.'

'I suppose it takes two to tango,' she admitted, sitting down.

'It certainly does. And what a dance it was while it lasted,' he joked, placing himself down next to her.

'It was,' she said, managing to raise a smile.

'So, when do you leave for London?'

'The car is due to arrive around five. Apparently, the motorway is full of roadworks and diversions. So, I could be waiting a while.'

As they had done many times before—they gazed into each other's eyes; it was the place where only they existed, in a world where nothing was rational. But Kean was quick to break free from the moment before it led to dangerous territories again.

'Rash was at the Cuban that night. He was watching us,' he reminded her.

'Yes, I remember. He must have always been watching me wherever I went—which really freaks me out.'

'So, maybe London is best.'

She stopped, thought for a second, and nodded. 'Yeah, I guess so.'

'Although I've been removed from the case, I promise you I won't stop until I find him.'

'Thank you,' she breathed.

Moving closer to her, he placed his hand on her upper arm, causing her to shiver with excitement. 'Well, I guess it's goodbye then.'

Not saying a word, she nodded.

I hope you catch him. He ruined my life, she thought. But then she realised that if it wasn't for Rash, she would never have met Kean.

'Going to miss you,' she said softly.

As he leaned forward to give her a kiss on the cheek, she turned and faced him; their lips touched lightly, so he kissed her on the lips instead—and she kissed him back— then their lips locked tightly together.

God, I already miss him, she thought.

Before she knew it, they were on his red leather sofa, all over each other with excitement.

'We shouldn't be doing this,' he whispered faintly into her ear, not sure if she even heard him. But nothing in the world could stop them.

He removed his shirt, as she did her leather jacket. She then slipped off her shirt and bra while she gently placed herself on his lap. She reminded him of one of those rodeo girls that rode bulls he saw on TV once—and God, didn't she look sexy in just her jeans.

He held her left breast delicately, leaned forward, and teased her nipple with his tongue making her tremble with pleasure. She then undid her belt and slowly removed her jeans and pants, and lay on top of him. *Riding the bull, was it?* Kean smiled with satisfaction.

When he leaned back, he noticed that the cold leather of the sofa was rough and stuck to his skin. For the first time, he admitted it was a mistake buying a leather one and wished he had bought the navy cloth instead. But still, this time making love felt so much better than the first. It felt more meaningful—maybe it was because they were more relaxed in each other's company—or perhaps because it was a farewell with emotions getting the better of them.

Later, they had one final kiss at the front door.

'What is it?' asked Daniela.

'It's nothing,' he replied, dismissively, looking emotional.

'If you don't tell me, then I'll be wondering what was wrong all the way to London—and probably won't sleep tonight,' she smiled.

He laughed. 'All right. I was wondering if this will develop into anything more. I mean, I know it's not ideal right now—but I'm mad about you!'

She stopped and stared deep into his eyes. Although she didn't say it, *I feel the same,* she thought.

'Being in a serious relationship with me is difficult,' she admitted.

'Because of your status?'

Daniela nodded; her eyes suddenly became teary. 'It has its consequences. My father is not the easiest person to get on with.'

Kean was just about to say something when Viola called Daniela.

'Miss Flores, where are you!? The car is here!' she said in a panicky voice.

'Shit! I didn't expect it to get here so fast! Okay—I put my bags outside my bedroom door. Please Viola, can you load them into the car for me?'

'Yes, Miss Flores,' she said, hanging up.

'It must be difficult having maids and butlers,' grinned Kean.

'It has its advantages,' said Daniela with a smile.

They held each other tight and had one last kiss before she headed out the front door.

Kean watched her from the window, walking swiftly away and disappearing down the road. He then called X, who, as always, was quick to answer.

'Inspector, I see you've been removed from the case. And yet you keep seeing the Ambassador's daughter. Interesting,' he said with smugness.

How the hell did he know that? wondered Kean.

'Rash needs to be found fast!' he told X.

'Maybe it will be a good idea to search his past first.'

'What do you mean?'

'He has no history. He just appeared from nowhere.'

'Impossible. He must have had a passport and A-level certificates to enter university.'

'You police are all the same—always satisfied with the first clue you find,' said X. 'And Inspector, one more thing.'

'What?'

'The Ambassador has sent a spy to keep an eye on Daniela. Luckily she outsmarted him and escaped through the back door to come to see you.'

'A spy?'

X let out a short laugh. 'You're playing with fire Inspector.'

After talking to X, Kean thought long and hard. He admitted that he needed to keep a distance from Daniela. That would be easy now that she was going to London. He needed to concentrate on the case. But who *was* Rash? He called Sergeant Reynolds to ask her if she had found anything relevant.

'I was just explaining to Inspector Griffith that I couldn't find any history on a Rashid Hassan Saadek. He seems to have fallen out of the sky!'

'Did you check again with the university? How about contacting his school?'

'All the documents are fake, Inspector! A person with that name didn't attend the school written on the certificate. All the A-level documents are fake too. The examination board is starting an investigation.'

'Incredible. We need to find a home address. He must have been living somewhere before Canterbury.'

'No home address. Only the Canterbury one!'

16

DANIELA arrived after a 30-minute brisk walk. She hugged Viola before getting into the black Mercedes with tinted windows. The driver, neatly dressed in a suit and a black tie, stood by the rear door, which he had open waiting for her. It was the first time Daniela had seen him but didn't feel the need to question where Jacob was, as his father's staff seemed to change in the blink of an eye.

'Guard the house while I'm gone, Viola,' she said jokingly.

'Madam, I've been given leave until further notice. I will visit my sister in Reading.'

'You take care now. I will miss you.'

'Thank you, madam. Likewise. You take care too.'

'There are bottles of water at the sides,' said the driver as he shut the door when Daniela was seated.

'Thank you,' she said, happy to see that the back of the vehicle was divided from the front, so she wouldn't be forced to engage in small talk with the driver.

She felt antisocial and miserable, wondering if what she was feeling was actually lovesickness. But there was more to it than that. The multiple murders around her made her feel grim. And Jack's death was the final straw. The image of Rash telling him to watch out for Harry flashed in her mind, giving her a chill. All the signs were there and she couldn't see them at the time—the way he used to look at her with his murderous shark-like eyes, and the strange way he acted whenever she used to visit Victor.

She took her phone out of her bag, praying a message had come from Kean telling her that Rash had been caught and there was nothing else to worry about—and that he missed her. She would tell the driver to take her straight back. But unfortunately, the only things on her mobile's screen were irrelevant notifications.

For a while, she took her mind off all the worries and got lost in the cyber world—looking at pictures posted by her friends and reading the cringeworthy comments and tweets. Then something else started bothering her. At first, she couldn't put her finger on it. The car started to sway as the driver started speeding when they reached the motorway.

Daniela looked up from her phone and saw that they were heading towards Dover. In disbelief, she stared out the window with her mouth open for a couple of seconds—maybe longer, until she leaned forward and knocked on the dark glass in front. There was no sound from the driver, who was easily going over ninety miles per hour now.

'Hey! What's going on!? Why aren't we headed towards London!?' Daniela cried anxiously, but the driver didn't answer and pressed harder on the gas.

'CAN YOU HEAR ME!' she tried again, this time a lot louder. 'HELLO?'

Daniela was just about to dial her father when the car came to a screeching stop on the hard shoulder. The driver opened the door, reached inside, and snatched the phone out of her hand, striking her hard across the face. Stunned by the burning sensation on her jaw, she felt tears spilling from her eyes as her head hit the seat. She heard the door shut and the driver's one open and close as he got inside and pulled out onto the motorway again.

'What do you want from me?' she managed, before passing out.

Once the computer had loaded, Kean logged into the police files. He always preferred working from his home computer where there were no distractions. Rash must have had a past. He couldn't have just fallen out the sky. It was a long shot but he started looking through the missing persons files. He always found it fascinating how many there were that hadn't been found, some dating back almost sixty years. He held the mouse firmly and scrolled down at a steady pace. He stopped when he saw the name Rashid Hassan Saadek. But this guy looked a lot older and had a pointier nose. In frustration, Kean exhaled a large breath and clicked on detailed search. He amended the dates so only missing persons from the last two years would show.

After searching for about fifteen minutes, he was about to give up, when he stopped and looked carefully at the profile photo of a young man. He had a slight lazy eye. The nose also seemed identical. The name read: Saleem Raza. Last seen: Oakwood Birmingham Mental Health Hospital.

The Inspector spilt the screen to compare a photo of Rash with the one of Saleem Raza—and froze when he saw both photos side by side. He had no doubt they were the same person.

'Unbelievable!' he muttered to himself.

Rash appeared more sensible and intelligent—with spectacles, a beard, nicely combed hair and a white shirt. He seemed like an academic—someone whose parents wouldn't complain if their daughter had dated him. Saleem, on the other hand, had a shaved head, he was frowning, wearing a black vest and a large chain around his neck, similar to the one worn by Mr. T. He looked completely unapproachable.

Kean called the police station and asked to be put through to Superintendent Lowe.

'Superintendent, I just found the true identity of Rashid Hassan Saadek!'

'Inspector Kean! Didn't I tell you that you're not on this case anymore!'

He was silent for a second.

'Come on then—who is he?'

'Check your email,' said Kean.

He listened to Michael Lowe hurriedly tapping and clinking on his computer's keyboard, impatiently trying to get into the email and download the file that Kean had sent him.

'I don't know how you do it!' Lowe said eventually, maybe a bit annoyed that Kean's help was always valuable.

'That explains why no one with the name of Rashid Hassan Saadek exists. His real name is Saleem Raza.'

'Incredible, absolutely incredible!' Lowe kept repeating. 'You're not going to let this case go, are you?'

'I'm sorry,' said Kean, softly and listened to Lowe take in a deep breath at the other end of the line.

'Listen, do what you have to do. But keep out of trouble!' he said before hanging up.

Kean smiled to himself and took another hard look at the pictures of Saleem and Rash on the spilt screen; at first glance they appeared to be different people, but those unfocused grey eyes had the same crazy look.

17

DR Fernando Mata had worked at the Stoke City Hospital for eight months when one of the nurses from the Gastroenterology department set him up on a blind date with her friend. Her name was Sarah Blunt, a psychologist at the Oakwood Birmingham Mental Health Hospital.

To his delight, she agreed to meet him in Stoke, so Fernando didn't have to drive to Birmingham and find out that the blind date might turn out to be a disappointment. But when he arrived at the Curry Palace, he was pleasantly surprised. Luckily, she was better looking than her friend, Jessica, the nurse from gastro who had set them up. She was a brunette, had her hair tied up in a ponytail, and had beautiful blue eyes. She was also athletic, just the way he liked them.

'So, Jessica tells me you're from Mexico,' she said with some level of enthusiasm.

'Originally, yes. I've been here since I was seven,' he said, taking a menu that was offered to him by the waiter.

'You're the first Mexican person that I've ever met. Isn't that crazy?' she said, opening her menu.

'What would you like to drink?' interrupted the waiter.

Fernando looked at his date and indicated for her to choose.

'A glass of white wine,' Sarah answered.

'Make that a bottle of Chardonnay,' Fernando told the waiter.

When the waiter thanked him and walked away, Fernando cast his attention back to Sarah. 'So, I'm the first ever Mexican, huh? That does make me feel special.'

She giggled and said that a patient she was seeing at the mental hospital was obsessed with Daniela Flores, who was the Mexican Ambassador's daughter.

'Really? Tell me more,' said Fernando with a curious look. 'What's the patient's name?'

'I can't tell you his name!' laughed Sarah. 'Patient confidentiality?'

'Sure, you can! I'm a doctor too, remember?'

'We'll see how the evening goes,' she winked. 'You'll have to gain my trust.'

'Is that how it is?' smiled Fernando cheekily.

The truth was that the evening went incredibly well. Fernando felt his Chicken Jalfrezi was spot on, the wine flowed down well, and Sarah wasn't just a pretty face. In fact, the evening went so well that they ended up in his house officer's accommodation tearing off each other's clothes. This was too easy for a snake like Fernando. What he didn't mention to her or Jessica was that it was his final day in Stoke. The day after, he would be leaving to start a new job at a hospital in London.

Being light-headed and under his charm, by the end of the night Sarah had told him everything about the patient who was obsessed with Daniela Flores.

After she left, Fernando dialled a number on his phone. A man answered.

'There better be a good reason why you're calling at this time,' he said.

'There is! You're gonna like this.'

'I'm listening. You better make it fast. Are you alone?'

'Yes, I'm alone. You made it clear that I shouldn't call you unless I was alone.'

'Good. Then tell me already!' sniffed the man.

'I've found someone who's obsessed with Daniela.'

There was a pause.

'Clarify what you mean by obsessed?'

'I mean obsessed—as in he's mad about her—to the level that he would kill to be with her.'

'Yeah? Who is it?' asked the man, showing a little more interest, but not too much so that Fernando wouldn't feel good about himself.

'His name is Saleem Raza. A patient at the Birmingham Oakwood Mental Health Hospital.'

'Really? And would he be interested in changing his identity?'

'If we promised to locate him close to Daniela, he would.'

'I'll get someone to check him out tomorrow. You better be right about this, Fernando. Otherwise, I'll make sure you get fed to the dogs!'

Fernando nervously laughed at the man's joke, but then suddenly stopped himself when he realised from his silence that he wasn't joking.

'From what his doctor said, Saleem Raza, sounds like just the man we're looking for!'

The man hesitated. 'And why would the doctor give information about his patient? Isn't it unethical?'

'*Her* patient,' smiled Fernando.

'You dog,' the man tutted with a slight laugh. Then with a serious tone added. 'You better pray this works.'

Fernando swallowed hard. *I better,* he thought to himself, nervously.

18

SERGEANT O'Leary called just as Kean was researching Saleem Raza. The Inspector was happy to see O'Leary calling. He had always been loyal and knew where his allegiances lay.

'Hello, O'Leary.'

'Inspector, there's been a further development in the case!' he said excitedly.

'Shouldn't you be telling this to Noel, instead?' the Inspector said.

'He's like a headless chicken,' replied O'Leary. 'Doesn't know whether he's coming or going. Anyone would think he's the star of some action movie.'

'Sounds about right. So, what's the new development?'

'Norman, the specialist IT technician, took in Rash's computer for examination.'

'And what did he find?'

'The suicide note was written on his computer, but get this—Rash didn't write it.'

It took Kean a moment for O'Leary's words to sink in. In all his years of policing, he had never encountered a case that fazed him as much as this one. He put it down to the fact that Canterbury was mainly a small uneventful city with just occasional cases of petty theft and the elderly complaining about noise created by the students. He wondered if this was the type of case he'd have to deal with regularly if he was based in a larger city. But even by their standards, this would be a major case. He was dealing with a serial killer—or killers.

'Are you okay, Inspector?' asked O'Leary, noticing Kean's silence.

'Yes, I am. I was just thinking. Is Norman positive that Rash didn't type the note?'

'He says that he's a hundred percent sure.'

Kean knew about the secret function available in the Word program that many people were oblivious to. It showed how much pressure was applied when pressing on the keys on the keyboard during typing and showed the individual user's typing pattern and timing. Norman told O'Leary that it didn't match Rash's typing style.

'Also, Inspector, I hear that Rash's true identity has been found,' added O'Leary. 'Just how do you do it?'

'It's called initiative. People just don't fall out of the sky. Everyone has a past if you dig deep enough.'

'Amazing, Inspector! Anyway, going back to the note, there are a couple of suspects who could have typed it.'

'Julie and Ron?'

'That's right. The two remaining housemates.'

'Do they possess computers?' Kean asked.

'They don't.'

'In that case, I would suggest that Ron's user account at the university is checked. If you don't get a result, get Julie to type a couple of sentences on Word to see if it matches the note.'

'Will do, Inspector. So, who do you think is behind all this?' asked O'Leary.

Judging by the tone of his voice, Kean felt like it was more of a plea for help. The case looked as if it could be heading for another dead end if no other evidence was found and the typing pattern did not match Ron's or Julie's.

'Without any strong evidence, it's hard to say. How about you, O'Leary?'

'To be honest, at first, I thought it was Daniela—and then Jose—and after he was killed, I was certain it was Rash. But now that he's disappeared—leaving behind what seems to be a mysterious suicide note, I'm at a loss, to be honest,' said O'Leary.

'There's something we're missing. It might be a good idea to look into Ron's and Julia's pasts too.'

'Inspector Griffith has already done that.'

'Any news?'

'Nothing too out of the ordinary. Except, Julia did have a tragic childhood.'

Kean was intrigued about Julia's past. O'Leary explained everything, starting from the car accident that killed her father when they were on the way to the cinema—which led to her uncle sending her to boarding school and then getting caught with drugs and ultimately being expelled.

A distant childhood memory suddenly came rushing back to Kean from when he was eight. Nizar, who was from Libya and whose surname Kean couldn't recall after all these years—was his best friend at the international school he attended in Hampstead. Nizar's father was an important businessman of some kind who had made massive investments across the United Kingdom. Kean remembered visiting Nizar's house in Bishop's Avenue. His jaw had dropped the moment the car pulled up outside the house. It was huge. One thing that had impressed Kean when he walked inside was the size of the TV. It reminded him of the cinema. He could probably fit ten of his TV screens into it; it was so massive. Then, on a dark winter's day at school, Kean recalled the classroom door swinging open and Mr Ellis, the headmaster, walking in—looking grim and off-colour. With sympathy, he stared at Nizar across the room, asking him to come with him. That was the last time Kean had ever seen Nizar.

A week later, Mrs Carry, the class teacher, explained that Nizar wouldn't be returning to school. And after a couple of months had passed—maybe longer, Kean's mother explained to him that Nizar's father had been involved in a fatal car accident. Kean knew all too well what that kind of psychological damage could do to a child.

'Actually, O'Leary, it is out of the ordinary,' he said, suddenly feeling sorry for Julie, just as he had felt for his best friend at the time.

Shortly after he'd hung up, Lowe called, sounding impatient and irritated, which was the norm for him. The Superintendent didn't believe in small talk and always got straight to the point. Maybe he didn't have the time due to his line of work and busy schedule—or perhaps it was the way he was brought up by a military family.

'Kean! A background check on Saleem Raza has been conducted. After talking to the West Midlands Police, it looks like an interesting breakthrough has been made. And I want you to follow it up!'

'What did you find?' asked Kean, laughing to himself that he had been reassigned to the case on a separate mission—which meant he didn't have to answer to Noel.

'Saleem's mother admitted that someone had helped him escape from the infirmary and used his uncle as a middleman,' explained Lowe.

'So, the plot thickens,' said Kean, bewildered. 'Why would anyone do such a thing?'

'That's what his mother is saying anyway. She's petrified, so she's been put under police protection. She thinks that they'll be coming for her next.'

Kean was convinced that the murders must have been connected to whoever had helped Saleem Raza escape. For a second, he wondered whether Ron or Julie had anything to do with it.

'I'll talk to the uncle to see if I can get anything out of him,' he said.

'You can't.'

Kean stopped for a moment. 'Why not?'

'Because he was shot dead a couple of months ago, which is why his sister, Saleem's mother, came forward and told the police that the uncle, Usman, was acting as the middleman. It is now believed that whoever helped Saleem escape shot Usman.'

'So, could the shooting be connected to the murders in Canterbury?'

'That's for you to find out,' grunted Lowe.

19

THE black Mercedes with the red, white and green Mexican flag flapping wildly on the vehicle's front right side entered Rayford Avenue, a quiet road a mile away from the city centre. Alberto sat restlessly at the back watching the block of maisonettes as several elderly faces, wrinkled and pale, stared back at him, curiously watching the car drive past from the windows.

Of course, most residents here are pensioners, he thought. *A perfect place to retire—away from the busy city life.*

His mind automatically switched back to his missing daughter.

The police had already spoken to Viola. And now she was going to get a second dose of questioning from the Ambassador—which she was dreading no doubt. The car parked in a vacant space opposite the maisonette that Alberto had been renting for Daniela. He stepped outside the vehicle and examined it for a while as he buttoned up his anorak. Each building was identical, containing a top and a bottom floor maisonette. He suddenly felt sick when he imagined the imposter vehicle parking at this very spot and taking his daughter away.

When he entered the building, he found Viola, who was off colour and trembling uncontrollably with fear.

'I'm sorry,' she burst out crying when she saw him.

The one thing Alberto couldn't stand was a crying woman. It made him uncomfortable. Expressionless, he produced a small packet of tissues from his anorak pocket, took one out and delicately handed it to her.

'Thank you,' she breathed, carefully taking it from his hand.

He turned and looked out of the large living room window, catching a glimpse of the parked car and the driver, Jacob, standing beside it waiting for him.

'You know Jacob,' he said casting his attention back to Viola.

Viola nodded. 'Yes,' she sniffed, wiping her tears with the tissue that Alberto had given her.

'And did you recognise the driver that came for Daniela?'

She stared at him blankly and slowly shook her head. *No.*

He raised a slight (but intimidating) grin.

'Then why the *hell* didn't you check who he fucking was? Why didn't you call the Embassy?'

'The car—' she stuttered, her Latin accent getting stronger the more she panicked. 'It was identical to the one outside. With the flag. And the driver was dressed in a black suit, similar to the one Jacob usually wears.'

'Did you talk to him?'

'I asked him if he was new. He said that he was.'

'Oh, well that was easy, wasn't it? And the police? What did they say?'

'I gave them a description of the driver.'

'Did you?' asked Alberto acrimoniously, feeling hot under the collar.

He fought hard not to lose it. He had a strong urge to blame and lash out at someone—but Viola seemed far too fragile—as if it was her own family member that was missing. It even made him feel sorry for her—almost.

'Is there anything else that I should know about? Anything that you aren't telling me?' he asked her calmly.

This time, Viola avoided eye contact. She seemed petrified as his imposing figure got so close that she could smell his aftershave—an aura that made her feel even more nervous for some reason—making her heart pound even faster.

'What is it?' he asked her.

As much as she wanted to get it off her chest, she had promised Daniela that she wouldn't say anything about Inspector Nicolas Kean to anyone.

'It's nothing,' Viola said, still looking down at the floor and avoiding eye contact.

'I see,' Alberto said, doubtfully.

He turned and allowed himself to fall backwards onto the sofa, transforming into a broken man—feeling sorry for himself. He reminded Viola of her own father after he and her mother had divorced.

Alberto demanded a glass of whisky, as his head fell back and he closed his eyes. 'No ice!' he added.

It wasn't long before he received a call from Inspector Noel Griffiths. Griffiths introduced himself to the Ambassador and reassured him that he would do everything he could to make sure Daniela was found, but first he wanted to meet Alberto in person when he heard that he was in Canterbury. Within fifteen minutes, he and O'Leary had arrived at the maisonette.

'The description that Viola gave was a bit hazy, but I know who abducted your daughter,' said Griffiths, smugly.

'Go on...' urged Alberto.

'His name is Saleem Raza—goes by the name of Rash. His height fits the description perfectly. He's six foot something. He's been obsessed with your daughter for a while and he's the prime suspect for all the killings, including the murder of Jose Perez.'

'Inspector—?' said O'Leary, from behind, looking concerned, but Noel just ignored him.

'Once we track down Saleem, we'll certainly find Daniela—'

'Inspector!?' O'Leary tried again, red faced.

'What is it, Sergeant O'Leary!? Can't you see that I'm trying to talk to Mr Flores?' Griffiths said in frustration.

'Inspector, what I've been trying to tell you for the last twenty minutes, since leaving the station, is that I've been informed by headquarters that Saleem Raza has been found dead.'

Noel Griffiths swallowed hard with an embarrassed look. 'Are you sure?'

'I'm positive,' answered O'Leary, casting a quick glance towards Alberto. And almost smirking to himself while he thought, *Try explaining this one to the Ambassador, Noel. You seemed so sure that Rash was the kidnapper!*

20

AN hour earlier, the Green family had been enjoying their Italian meal at *Little Roma* by the river, but it had turned out to be a nightmare. Being a pescatarian, George Green opted for the anchovy and artichoke pizza, while his wife Cynthia had ordered a plain salmon salad. Jamie, their six-year-old son, was treated to what he always loved—the pepperoni special, his favourite. The table across the room became vacant.

'Daddy! Look! There's a free table by the window! Let's sit there! I want to watch the ducks and the fishes!'

'It's *fish*, Jamie, not *fishes*. And we're not changing tables now. We already have our food,' said George, biting a sizable piece of the pizza, as a bit of artichoke fell onto his plate and then bounced onto the floor.

'Please, daddy! Mummy, say something!' begged Jamie, but they just rolled their eyes.

After a couple of minutes of being ignored by his parents, Jamie stood up.

'Fine! I'm just going to have to go and have a quick peek outside!' he mumbled, marching across the room towards the window like a soldier on a mission.

'Jamie! Finish your pizza first, my dear!' Cynthia called after him—but he ignored her.

Walking around the table, he headed towards the window and looked outside. A cold draught of air crept through the edges of the windowpane, making him involuntarily rub his hands together. Here, the river was at its narrowest. The window faced a red brick wall, which was only about four metres away from the restaurant.

It wasn't long before Jamie returned to the table to join his parents. They were in such a deep conversation that they didn't notice that his face had gone pale with shock. The kid had transformed from a red-faced chatterbox to a silent phantom. Maybe, at first—although they were oblivious to it—it was somewhat of a luxury for George and Cynthia Green, because they were having a conversation with no interruptions from Jamie. But Jamie just sat there, staring into space, extremely disturbed by what he had seen floating in the river a few moments ago. Even for an adult, it would have been too much to take in, but it was absolutely traumatising for a six-year-old.

'I want to replace the garden bench by the pond,' said Cynthia, attacking a piece of salmon with her fork.

'What's wrong with the one we already have, dear?' asked George, as sweat trickled down his large forehead. 'I seem to recall that it cost me an arm and a leg!'

Cynthia rolled her eyes and said, 'Did you see the one in John and Mary's garden? It's so much nicer than ours …Jamie, are you going to eat that last slice of pizza? You've been staring at it for the last ten minutes! Jamie—are you okay? Jamie—why aren't you talking?'

'In …th …the …riv …riv …river,' Jamie stuttered, pointing towards the window with his trembling hand.

'Stop it, Jamie! There's nothing in the river,' she said, getting up to take a look to prove to him there was nothing there except for his weird six-year-old imagination. Cynthia calmly walked over to the window and looked down at the river. For a second or so, she was silent—then she suddenly screamed a scream so full of fear that it made a passing waitress almost drop her tray of drinks.

After another ten minutes had passed, the place was swarming with police, reporters, and a variety of curious onlookers hanging around the scene, with murmurs going through the large crowds outside.

It's The Silent Killer! The Silent Killer has struck again!

21

AT first, Kean was not successful in contacting Sarah Blunt, who had been Saleem Raza's doctor at the time when he'd escaped from the Oakwood Birmingham Mental Health Hospital. Although Kean got put through to Blunt's assistant, she simply transferred the call back to the switchboard. When he asked for Blunt's mobile number, the switchboard had refused to give it out saying it was unethical, and on the phone, he couldn't prove that he was a policeman.

Shortly after he hung up feeling defeated, a call came through from O'Leary, who sounded flustered.

'Inspector, Daniela has been kidnapped ...and also Rash has been found dead in the river!'

'What!?' asked Kean, his voice going up an octave.

'I'm just about to meet up with Noel. We were supposed to be talking to Alberto Flores, but now that there's a crime scene, we'll probably go there first!'

Kean could hardly breathe. It was too much information to take in all at once. *Daniela, kidnapped? Rash, dead? Never mind about Rash! Daniela has been kidnapped!*

'How did she get taken?' he asked.

O'Leary noticed the pain in his voice.

'She was last seen being driven away in a black Mercedes.'

'By the Ambassador's vehicle?'

'She thought it was, but the real one turned up half an hour later. Listen, I have to go, Inspector. Noel is coming.'

Never before in his career had Kean panicked so much. After hanging up, he stood up and walked around the room with his hands on his head. He then sat down and gazed out of the window, feeling lost. Once again, he realised how deep he had fallen for Daniela and how personal this case had become for him. He had to find Daniela before she got hurt …or even worse!

Rash was obsessed with Daniela. And now Rash was dead— and Daniela kidnapped. There's definitely something being overlooked. Can Ron and Julie be behind this? But what would their motive be? There needs to be a motive. And besides, there's no solid evidence!

As much as he was tempted to pay Julie and Ron a visit, he went to the crime scene instead, and called X on the way.

'Long time, Inspector,' crackled X's distorted voice.

'You must know something!'

'She got into a car similar to the one the Mexican Embassy uses. But apart from that, I've got nothing for you.'

'Then it should be possible to trace the car through the motorway cameras,' said Kean with a sudden glimmer of hope in his voice.

'It seems that this was an intricately planned operation. The driver must have removed the flag and even the number plates at some point.'

'Any idea who might be behind this? Are the murders linked with Daniela's kidnapping?'

'This wasn't just done by some disturbed kid who went around drugging people. It seems that unleashing Saleem Raza was part of a larger plan.'

'What do you mean?'

'With all the killings, the murder of Jose and the kidnapping of Daniela, who just happens to be the Mexican Ambassador's daughter, it seems that there's a mastermind behind all this.'

'So, what you are saying is Saleem Raza was manipulated—'

'As well as a few others, no doubt,' interrupted X.

'But why would anyone go to such great lengths?' asked Kean, pressing harder on the gas pedal once the traffic in front of him had cleared.

'Difficult to say. It could be an attack on Alberto Flores.'

'But so many innocent people died unnecessarily!'

'Yes, all of them got close to Daniela.'

Kean swallowed hard, remembering the crow that had been shoved into his exhaust. He was a definite candidate for *The Silent Killer*.

'Pray that there will be some kind of a ransom note soon, Inspector.'

The Inspector paused for a couple of seconds.

'And if there isn't?' he asked, seeking a parking spot at the carpark near Westgate.

'Then expect the worse,' replied X, his words sending chills down the Inspector's spine. 'Alberto's spy. There is a chance that he might have followed the car.'

'If that's the case, surely Alberto would have mentioned something by now.'

'Unless he wants to keep it on the low.'

By the time Kean had found a free parking spot and arrived at the scene, the body had already been removed from the water. He looked around for O'Leary and Noel, but they were nowhere to be seen. He wondered if they went to see Alberto Flores first. Maybe he would mention something about the spy following the car and Daniela's possible location.

A couple of splats of diluted blood were on the floor near the body, which was covered up. Pamela was kneeling down, holding a cotton bud to one of them, taking a sample.

'What's with the blood?' Kean asked.

'Inspector, this is getting out of control! In all my years in the service, there have never been so many murder cases in a row as there have been in the last couple of months!' she said, carefully unscrewing the lid of the test tube before dropping the cotton bud inside.

'So, do we know the cause of death?'

'The victim received two hard blows to the back of the head. He must have been unconscious when entering the water.'

Kean could hear Sergeant Rickson questioning a couple and their son, who apparently was the first to spot the body floating in the river.

'Can you check for Ro—'

'Rohypnol? I will. And just a reminder that there wasn't any in Jose Alves's system. So, there's nothing to say that there'll definitely be in his,' said Pamela, gesturing at Rash's body.

'Thank you,' said Kean.

His phone rang, vibrating in his jacket's inner pocket.

'Inspector Nicolas Kean?' asked a women's voice.

'Speaking, how can I help you?'

'I'm Dr Sarah Blunt. You left your number with the hospital. I was told that you've been looking for me.'

'Yes, I have. I wanted to ask you a couple of questions regarding Saleem Raza, a patient of yours who escaped from Oakwood,' said Kean, swiftly moving away from the crowd and finding himself a quiet spot. Until forensics had proved that Rash was indeed Saleem Raza, he didn't want to mention his death.

'Yes, I did look after him for a month. What do you want to know?'

'Did you suspect anything before he escaped?'

'No, I didn't.'

Did he get any visitors?'

'Only his uncle who used to visit him once a week.'

'Usman?'

Sarah paused for a second. 'Yes, that's right. Usman.'

'When visiting Saleem, did Usman ever bring anyone with him to the hospital?'

'Not that I can recall.'

'How about the cameras? Didn't they show anything?'

'All the cameras were down the day he escaped.'

'That's convenient,' sighed Kean. 'So, there wasn't any suspicious activity at the hospital before he disappeared?'

She was silent again, and Kean sensed that she wanted to tell him something.

'What is it?' he asked.

'Actually, a couple of days before he disappeared, I had dinner with a doctor who was working in Stoke at the time. He seemed very interested in Saleem.'

'In what way?' Kean asked eagerly.

'He was interested in Saleem's obsession with Daniela Flores, the Mexican Ambassador's daughter.'

Kean's heart started beating faster. 'What was his name?'

'Fernando Mata.'

'Mexican?'

'Yes …good guess.'

Kean took Mata's number.

'Do me a favour,' said Sarah, sounding slightly irritated.

'A favour?'

'When you talk to Mata, tell him that he's a jerk.'

22

JAMES French was having his mid-morning coffee in the Oakwood Birmingham Mental Health Hospital security office when there was a knock at the door. A well-dressed young man flashed his IT department badge at him. The name under his photo read Robert Rook.

'How can I help you?' asked French.

'Just need to do an update to the program,' replied Rook.

French was just about to ask him why he hadn't been notified beforehand but then stopped himself from doing so.

Why bother? What difference will it make? Just enjoy your coffee and biscuits, he thought. *Although the IT department usually sends a notification email about updates, it must have been overlooked.*

'Sure. Come in.' he said eventually, inviting Rook in.

He nodded and strolled in as French took his coffee and packet of ginger crunch biscuits, and placed himself at the back of the room, while Rook stationed himself in front of the multiple monitors.

'How long will you be? I can't take my eyes off the patients for too long,' said French, as he scanned the sports section in one of the tabloids on the table.

'About five minutes,' answered Rook, going into the settings file and tapping restart.

As all the monitors went blank, Rook turned and had a quick peek at French, who was munching on a ginger biscuit while focusing hard on the paper.

Firmly holding onto his phone, Rook hurriedly typed and sent a message: *Cameras are down.*

A thumbs up reply came straightaway. After another two minutes, he received another message: *Done. Get out fast!*

Rook got up and hurried towards the door.

French was now fully engrossed in his coffee and biscuits, lost in the world of the daily sports news. Just as Rook was exiting the door, he heard French call 'One minute,' from behind.

Rook stopped cold, his heart pounding.

'Say hi to Frasier from me!'

Relieved, Rook nodded without looking back, swiftly closing the door behind him, and disappearing down the corridor.

A minute later, two men wearing white lab coats and an IT worker got into a grey car and drove off, and within three minutes, the monitors were back on in the security station. After five minutes had passed, the alarm was raised when a patient named Saleem Raza was reported missing from his room. The entire building and the area within a 10-mile radius of the hospital were thoroughly checked. The search continued for a couple of weeks, but Saleem Raza was never seen again.

The hospital management ensured that information about the IT imposter was kept hidden. That kind of incident would surely ruin the hospital's reputation. James French was relieved from his job as security guard with no questions asked.

As for the two doctors and the IT technician who had gotten into the grey car and driven away, they were only seen by a couple of witnesses whose description of them was vague. They could have been anyone in a busy private hospital like Oakwood.

23

IT was all over the morning news. The Mexican Ambassador's daughter had been kidnapped, making Canterbury a field day for reporters. The President of Mexico made a personal call to Alberto Flores, while the Mexican government closely monitored the investigation.

Kean was in the office trying to get information on Fernando Mata—whose number was no longer registered—when he received a call from Pamela.

'The victim's file name has now been changed to Saleem Raza,' Pamela told him.

'You found his true identity then.'

'All the documents with the name Rashid Hassan Saadek are fake, just like you said. No such person exists.'

'At least Saleem Raza has been found. But it doesn't explain why he's been killed,' said Kean, scribbling circles with his pen in his notebook—something he did when he was overthinking—perhaps also going around in circles in his head.

'The two blows to the back of his head were possibly inflicted by some kind of wooden kitchen roller. They came in at an angle from the lower left, which means the person who did it was left-handed and also shorter than the victim,' explained Pamela.

Kean's circles got faster and more intense as he pressed the pen harder. 'Very technical. Could it have been a female?' he asked.

'Possibly, but then again, the victim is taller than your average male.'

A couple of minutes after the call from Pamela, there was a knock on the door. It was O'Leary. He had information regarding the suicide note found next to the Rohypnol and the notebook. It was printed using one of the student's user accounts at the college library. Her name is Fiona Riding. A second-year Irish student from Cork who is studying nursing. She logged into her account at 14:30 and forgot to log out again. At 15:36, the letter was uploaded by a USB stick and printed. At that time, Fiona claimed that she was at a sociology lecture. Her story checked out. She was in a lecture.

'So, any idea who typed it? Could it have been Saleem?' asked Kean.

Although O'Leary had memorised the report, he was looking through it, just to be sure of the facts.

'According to the IT forensics investigations department, the letters on the left side of the keyboard on

Rash's computer—where the original note was typed—were pressed harder. So, the person who typed the note must have been left-handed. Rash—I mean, Saleem was right-handed. Also, the typing pattern was significantly different from his. One that is typically seen in female typing. Saleem definitely didn't type this letter,' explained O'Leary, holding up a copy of the supposed suicide note.

Kean almost jumped out of his chair, which shocked O'Leary as he had never seen him this excited before.

'The person who killed Saleem is the same person who wrote the note!'

'How can you be so sure, Inspector?' asked O'Leary.

'I spoke to Pamela earlier. The autopsy report states that Saleem was hit on the head by a left-handed person. Because of the angle at which he was struck, it indicates that they were shorter than him—perhaps a female.'

'Very good Inspector! Shall I run this by Noel?' asked O'Leary.

'I'm sure he'll figure it out for himself.'

The Inspector thought hard, trying to remember the first time he'd visited 26 East Gate Drive. Julie was smoking. She was seated at the far-right side of the kitchen when he had entered, holding her cigarette with her hand closest to the wall—her left hand. Then something else suddenly occurred to him about the way Julie and Ron had regularly appeared on the news, giving interviews about the murders. Julie, in particular, seemed overenthusiastic about them and appeared to always want to be in the limelight.

Her voice echoed in Kean's head. *We were actually going to report Victor as missing today!*

'Sure, you were!' grunted Kean to himself as he was driving.

He suddenly entered a state of panic. What would happen if he was too late to save Daniela? Everyone was driving extra slowly, it frustrated him that this always happened whenever he was in a hurry

'*Fuck this!*' he breathed, winding down the window and whacking on the portable siren.

Julie and Ron had no idea that he wasn't in charge of the case anymore, and they didn't need to know either. When he arrived, he rang the doorbell and waited, but no one answered, so he desperately knocked on the door— loudly. Still, there was no answer.

As he was returning to the car, he received a call from X. Fernando Mata had been located. He was now working in the Gastroenterology Department at St Thomas' Hospital in London.

After speeding up to London, the Inspector found himself stuck in heavy traffic in the centre of the city. It turned dark and miserable as rain pinged hard off the car's roof and windscreen. A procession of red London buses swiftly passed by on the bus and taxi lane to his left, while Kean impatiently tapped his index fingers on top of the steering wheel, waiting for the cars in front to start moving. It was at times like this that he appreciated living away from the city.

He hoped Mata was there, otherwise, it would end up being a wasted day. He prayed that Fernando Mata had information that would be the key to finding Daniela. Eventually, the hospital came into view, and it wasn't long before he turned into the car park. The rain slowed, but the ground was wet with a new formation of puddles.

He hurried through the large sliding doors and up to the reception and flashed his badge at the lady behind the desk. He asked her where he could find Dr Fernando Mata. She gave him directions to the Gastroenterology Department with a curious look, but told him that he needed to hurry as it was nearing one o'clock, so Dr Mata would leave for lunch soon.

Kean took the lift to the 11th floor and followed the signs to Northumberland Ward. A young nurse at the front desk paged Dr Mata and told the Inspector that he was just seeing a patient. Kean walked up to a nearby window and took in the beautiful view. The tranquil water of the River Thames sparkled green and blue, welcoming the small droplets of rain. Next to the river, the London Eye slowly turned, with tourists catching a view of London from above.

'How can I help you,' asked a man with a deep voice from behind the Inspector.

Kean turned and faced him. He had a stethoscope around his neck, was tanned with straight black hair and certainly appeared to be Mexican. He looked worn-out like he was fed up of life, with bags under his dark eyes.

'Dr Mata? I'm Inspector Nicolas Kean,' said the Inspector, raising his badge. 'I came to ask you a couple of questions about Saleem Raza's disappearance from the Oakwood Birmingham Mental Health Hospital a couple of months ago. I think it might be connected to the kidnapping of Daniela Flores, the Mexican Ambassador's daughter.'

'Saleem Raza's disappearance and Daniela Flores?' repeated Mata, his eyes widening after each word.

'That's right, I believe you might have some information for me.'

It was at that moment that Kean witnessed something that in all his years in the police force, he'd never experienced before—a doctor pushing him to the floor and then sprinting away. Kean quickly got up and ran after him.

'Quick! Call for security!' he cried while running past the terrified nurse stationed at the front desk of the ward. He called for backup as he ran out onto the corridor. Mata was already at the far end running fast—getting away.

'*Bloody hell!*' Kean breathed to himself as he sprinted after him.

Mata hurriedly pressed on the elevator buttons, but he didn't have time to wait, so he carried on running and disappeared through the fire exit door.

Kean raced after him, and when he went through the fire exit, he initially headed down the stairs, but then realised that Mata wasn't heading in that direction at all. He was going up.

Nice try! thought Kean as he followed him up, taking two steps at a time.

He heard a clunk from above as a gush of chilly wind blew down the stairs. Kean guessed that he had gone through the metal door leading out to the roof, three floors above the Gastroenterology Department. He wondered what the point of his actions was. Did he think that being chased to the roof wouldn't get him caught? He was a doctor, so he must have had some initiative. But then again, even the most intelligent people do the most outrageous things when cornered—and Fernando Mata certainly was. He probably didn't expect that anyone would have connected him to Saleem escaping and Daniela being kidnapped. Certainly not on this day or any other.

Twenty seconds later, Kean reached the metal door, pushed on the handle, and stumbled out onto the roof, where the wind was so strong that it was a challenge to move forward. Mata ran towards the far ledge—his white coat flapping uncontrollably—and occasionally lost his balance in the intense gale. Breathless, Kean sprinted towards him.

Mata reached the ledge, climbed on it, stopped, and looked back at Kean.

'PUT YOUR HANDS UP AND GET DOWN FROM THERE!' Kean yelled, trying to project his voice through the wind. He dug up the keys for the handcuffs attached to his belt from his pocket.

'I SAID HANDS UP!' he repeated, getting closer.

Mata hesitated, looking across at the ledge of the other building—trying to calculate whether he could make the four-metre jump. On any other day—on a day that there was no storm—he would have given himself a good chance. But even then, he probably wouldn't take the risk if he wasn't getting chased.

'STOP! DON'T DO IT!' yelled Kean, who was now almost within arm's reach.

Taking a deep breath, Mata had to make a split decision. He thrust his body as far as it would take him to reach the other side. The wind blew harder, and time seemed to stop. As Mata was carried further along to the right by the strong gale, like a white feather gliding through the wind, Kean watched in horror. With a loud, desperate scream, he then disappeared over the edge.

Kean froze for a second, shocked at what he had just witnessed, then raced towards where Mata had jumped. By the time he looked down, Mata's body was on the pavement below, with a pool of blood spreading from beneath his cracked skull. Screams and sirens echoed from far below as a shocked crowd formed around the body.

Shaken and disappointed, Kean walked back inside to report the unfortunate incident to the Met. Why was Mata so desperate to run? It was clear he was hiding something.

24

WHEN Daniela came round, she shivered uncontrollably. It was cold and damp and almost too dark to see, but slowly, her eyes became accustomed to it. She appeared to be in a large storage room—or a warehouse. She tried to free herself, but her hands were tied tightly onto a railing behind her. She sat helplessly on the floor—her jaw was still sore from being struck.

The place was eerie—as if someone was watching her from behind the stacks of what appeared to be large cargo boxes. She scanned the room, trying to make out the letters printed on the boxes. The wind whistled outside while a dog barked in the distance. There was a dripping noise close by which sounded like it was coming from a tap.

Taking in a deep breath, she gathered up her courage, 'HELLO!? WHERE AM I? WHAT DO YOU WANT FROM ME!' she cried out.

Suddenly, something shuffled to her right, making her scream out in fear. In the darkness, she could make out a figure of a man sitting in a puddle with his head tilted to the side—covered by a cloth bag. There were splatters of blood on his shirt and jeans, and (muddy) white trainers. She tried to keep calm, but was shaking uncontrollably.

'Are you okay?' she called, choking on her words.

The man let out a feeble moan. She focused hard at him and realised that the dripping sound wasn't coming from a tab. It was the dripping of blood. Blood that he was lying in—*his* blood!

She started panicking further—her bag was missing, and she had no idea where her phone was. Did the driver take it, or did it fall on the ground somewhere? She couldn't remember ever feeling so frightened in her life. She was sure this was a feeling most people never experienced in their lives, unless they were faced with great danger (the danger of death)—like passengers on a plane that was going down—or someone who had been shot or stabbed. The phrase *life flashing before your eyes* suddenly made more sense to her. Being kidnapped by a killer isn't something that anyone imagines would ever happen to them. It was the uncertainty that made her panic—not knowing what the killer's intention was.

She tried hard to free her hands again, but the more she did, the tighter the rope squeezed her wrists together.

She waited—time passed—the temperature dropped …the cold became unbearable.

An indeterminable time later, she anxiously looked up when she heard footsteps approaching. A slim female figure emerged from the darkness, shining a torch into her face. When she came closer, Daniela recognised her instantly.

'Julie?' she breathed, condensation coming out of her mouth.

Julie walked up and grimly stared down at her.

'Hello, Daniela,' she said, coldly. 'You look surprised to see me!'

'Why would you do such a thing?' asked Daniela, her words barely coming out.

'You don't recognise me, do you, bitch.'

Daniela focused hard on her—then shook her head, *no*. She always thought there was something off about Julie—something not quite right. Her voice certainly sounded familiar, but she never really questioned it. She would have remembered someone loudmouthed and rude like Julie.

'Well, let me refresh your memory!' Julie, leaned closer and slowly stroked Daniela's hair, gently running her hand down her cold cheek in a seductive way. 'Does Steve Redford ring a bell? Six years ago? Lower-sixth? And a fat girl with glasses?'

'Julie from school?' mumbled Daniela in shock.

'Ding-dong!' sang Julie making a bell sound, then grabbed Daniela's hair, and tugged it hard. 'That's right! The fat girl with glasses who *everyone* used to pick on …making her life a living fucking hell! But look at me now! I look good, don't you think?'

Daniela tried to nod but Julie's grip on her hair was too tight. She did indeed look good, but her character had definitely changed for the worse, she thought.

'Let go of my hair!' begged Daniela, helplessly.

'Give me a good reason why I should!'

'I always stood up for you!' Daniela said, tears pouring down her cheeks as Julie sadistically tightened her grip even more.

'Yes—you did. And I thought an angel had come to save me from those fucking bullies. But then Steve Redford—' she stopped and started reminiscing.

Letting go of Daniela's hair, she stood up, and stared into space. Daniela sighed with relief as her hair was freed, but the fact she couldn't rub her head to relieve the pain caused her almost as much discomfort as the actual grip, as tears ran down from her eyes.

'Steve did it as a bet! He wasn't interested in you!' she wept.

'But he kissed me—'

'It was a bet, Julie! A fucking bet!'

'Then you started dating him! You were meant to be my friend!' said Julie in a sweet, but patronising voice.

'I found about the bet later. I had no idea! I swear to God!'

'LIAR!' spat Julie.

The person whose head was covered started to twitch and groan again—like a sound that zombies make in movies.

'Who's that?' asked Daniela, sensing the fear in her own voice.

'Someone had to be sacrificed,' Julie said with an evil smirk. 'Now, excuse me as I have some unfinished business to attend to.'

She walked over to the person lying on the floor and picked up something shiny, as her torn jeans swayed freely from under her fitted leather jacket with a large white *peace* logo on the arm. A second later, Daniela realised what Julie was holding. It was a tiny saw—the type used to cut small pieces of wood during craft classes. Leaning down, she lifted the cloth, exposing the man's face. Daniela's eyes widened with horror when she saw who it was.

'Ron!?' she cried in disbelief.

Ron moaned—his face was swollen, and his eyes were unfocused—puffed and droopy—reminding Daniela of Lurch from the Addams Family. Julie grabbed his little finger tightly and pulled his hand closer to her. Then she began to saw. It took Daniela a while to register what was happening, and when she did, the cracking noise caused by the metal breaking through the bone of the finger made her so nauseous that she could hardly breathe. Ron didn't scream, but just moaned and tried to mumble a couple of words.

'It's amazing what Rohypnol can do,' admitted Julia, as she worked the saw back and forth. She seemed so relaxed that it was as if she was cutting through wood.

'You know, I tried earlier, but the drug hadn't kicked in yet. All the screaming ...can't stand the fucking screaming!'

'HELP! SOMEBODY—PLEASE HELP!' screamed Daniela.

'Don't you get it? Scream all you want. No one can hear you here!' hissed Julie.

You fucking psycho, thought Daniela, but kept the comment to herself.

'Why Julie? Why are you doing this?' she asked instead, her voice trembling with fear.

Julie gave Ron's finger a final tug, tearing it from the last piece of flesh that was holding it together. With the saw in one hand and Ron's little finger in the other dripping with blood, she walked past Daniela.

'All will be revealed soon,' she said, walking down the hall and disappearing into the darkness.

<h1 style="text-align:center">25</h1>

SUPERINTENDENT Michael Lowe sat in silence for a while, examining the papers on his desk before looking up at Kean. He removed his reading glasses, folded them and gently placed them on the table.

'So, just like that, he fell to his death?' he asked with a suspicious look.

Kean nodded. 'He looked petrified when I brought up the subject of Saleem escaping from Oakwood and Daniela's kidnapping. I could see it in his eyes that he knew something.'

'All we need to do is scratch the surface, and we'll find ourselves in the middle of mafia crossfire,' stated Lowe, who suddenly realised he had no idea how he would handle this. He didn't have enough experience to deal with a case this delicate.

'Let me tell *you* something you don't know,' he said eventually. 'Something that Inspector Noel managed to dig up.'

Kean listened curiously, waiting to see what Noel had *managed to dig up*. The fact that Noel could solve anything was unthinkable. The guy was an idiot, and Kean always wondered how on earth he'd slipped through the net to become an inspector.

'Fernando Mata and Alberto Flores are cousins—were cousins.'

'Cousins!?'

'That's right! *Cousins*,' repeated Lowe.

Kean suddenly felt irritated that he couldn't get any information from Mata, but Noel had been praised for establishing the connection between Fernando Mata and Alberto Flores.

'Alberto must know something. This is too much of a coincidence,' said Kean. 'We need to interview him—'

'*That* won't be necessary. Noel and O'Leary have already spoken to him.'

'And did they find anything useful?'

'He claims he hasn't seen or spoken to Mata in years.'

'Is he telling the truth?'

Lowe thoughtfully scratched the back of his head. 'We need to keep a close eye on the Ambassador. It's a long shot, but for all we know, the kidnapping could've been staged.'

That's ridiculous, thought Kean, but instead, he answered, 'Yes, Superintendent.'

When returning to his office, Kean bumped into Pamela. She had her hair tied in a bun and was wearing reading glasses, giving her an authoritative look. Beneath her white lab coat, she wore a navy-blue miniskirt that matched her high-heeled boots. As always, she was patrolling the corridors of the police station, carrying reams of paperwork tucked beneath her arm, which were mostly forensic reports.

'Pamela, what brings you to my neck of the woods?' asked Kean.

'Can we talk in your office?' she said—despite her serious appearance, she managed to return a slight smile.

'Sure.'

When they were in his office, Pamela placed the papers on his desk and then picked one of them out and slid it towards Kean.

'Just look at the volume of Rohypnol found in Saleem Raza's system,' she said, pointing at the recorded numbers printed on the autopsy report.

Kean's eyes widened. 'How many pills did he have to take to reach that volume?'

Pamela took a deep breath in. 'Between eight or nine.'

She looked deep into his eyes, and Kean knew what she was thinking as he held her deep blue gaze. She was an attractive girl and would have been a good catch, but no one could ever take Daniela's place.

'Thank you. This information will be …vital,' he said, clearing his throat and breaking the gaze.

'You're welcome, Inspector,' Pamela breathed, trying to control the speed of her heartbeat. In reality, her feelings for him went way back, but this was the first time she had managed to get his attention.

Victory, she thought. *Nick gave me a look!*

But little did she know that the feeling wasn't mutual. All Kean could think about in his anxious state was Daniela.

She was just about to say something when there was a loud knock at the door. It was O'Leary. Kean didn't recognise his knocking this time—it was loud and impatient—and when O'Leary walked in, he seemed rushed and flustered.

'Inspector! The kidnapper sent a parcel!'

Kean and Pamela looked at him in shock.

Wait? A parcel? What parcel? Usually, the kidnapper sends a letter or makes a phone call asking for the ransom! That's the way it has always worked, Kean told himself in his head.

'What was in it?' he asked.

'A letter …and a finger,' answered O'Leary grimly.

'A finger?' repeated Pamela with a lost look.

'That's right! An amputated finger!'

'Is it Daniela's?' asked Kean hesitantly, looking pale at the thought.

'Actually, I can't say. It's been sent to a lab in London for examination. As has the letter.'

'What does the letter say?' asked Kean.

O'Leary took his phone out from his trouser pocket and located the picture of the letter. He then started reading it with a theatrical voice.

Dear Alberto Flores,
For the time being, your daughter is safe. If you want to see her again, then there are two demands that you must carry out.
The first one is that you immediately resign from your position as ambassador, quietly, with no questions asked.
The second is that 10 million pounds in cash must be left by you in person at the flag side of the cloister garden where the son of a merchant was once violently murdered at the altar.
You have until 10pm on the date of 29 December.
Any police presence anywhere near the building will get your daughter killed! If you fail to execute these demands, your beloved daughter will share the same fate as the merchant's beloved son at the same place and on the same date.
Don't forget, she can lose more than just a finger!

No one spoke for at least a minute, but it seemed much longer.

'So, whose son violently died at the alter?' asked Pamela, eventually breaking the silence.

O'Leary raised his hands, indicating that he had no idea. 'We need to have all the churches in the area thoroughly checked,' he said.

Kean's face suddenly lit up.

'Of course!' he breathed, as he rushed to his computer.

Pamela and O'Leary eagerly followed him and stood close behind, watching him type the words *Thomas Becket's Death* into Google. The screen filled up with links about Thomas Becket.

At the top was a short paragraph which read: *Thomas Becket was the son of a merchant who became the Archbishop of Canterbury during the reign of Henry II. He was violently murdered at the altar of Canterbury Cathedral, December 29, 1170.*

'Bingo!' said Kean with a satisfied look. 'The cloister garden is inside the cathedral grounds!'

'Of course! Thomas Becket was executed at the cathedral! I remember learning about that in history lessons at school. Good work, Inspector! I'll let London know straight away!' said O'Leary.

'I wouldn't have a clue. I used to fall asleep during history lessons,' said Pamela with an embarrassed smile.

'We've got four days to try to locate him. Let me know what the forensics unit in London finds regarding the finger and letter,' said Kean.

'Will do, Inspector!'

26

THE wipers were set on full, working hard, washing the heavy rain out of the way and making the motorway ahead more visible. As always, the traffic was heavy.

'*Is everyone bloody going to London?*' said Alberto under his breath as he ran through the unexpected interrogation in his mind—an ordeal he was not expecting when he came down to Canterbury to seek his daughter. Her disappearance was bad enough without having to deal with any false accusations. Both the policemen had tried hard to dig for information but they were barking up the wrong tree, especially Inspector Noel Griffiths, who Alberto thought was a first-class idiot.

But they were the least of his worries. The fact that Fernando Mata was somehow involved in Daniela's disappearance deeply worried Alberto. He still couldn't get over the fact he was dead. He had tried to convince the two policemen that he hadn't talked to Fernando for more than five years. And even that was a brief encounter. Inspector Noel hadn't seemed too convinced, but Sergeant John O'Leary appeared to be more lenient.

A call came through from Veronica. She sounded nervous. 'Darling! A parcel! A parcel came by post in your name!'

'Did security give it a thorough check?'

'Yes, they did. Shall I open it?' she asked, anxiously.

'No, wait! As it's in my name, I should open it.'

'Darling?'

'Yeah?'

'Do you think it's from …you know—'

'The kidnappers? I dunno. Do the police know about it?'

'No, shall I inform them—'

'No! Let's see what it is first before we get them involved.'

After he hung up, he ordered Jacob to step on the gas.

By the time they arrived at the Flores mansion in St John's Wood, the sun was out, and it turned out to be a pleasant afternoon outside. However, inside the Flores household, the atmosphere wasn't as pleasant.

As Alberto stepped out of the car and walked towards the house, he heard the clicking of cameras and muttering. He turned to look and saw a couple of men standing on the property walls, taking his picture.

'GET OUTTA HERE OR I'LL CALL THE POLICE!' he yelled at them. They rapidly disappeared over the other side.

'Bloody paparazzi!' he muttered angrily to himself as he paced up to the front door, turned the key, and walked inside.

Veronica was sitting on the sofa at the far end, next to the fireplace, holding a glass of vodka-tonic. On the granite table in front of her was a wide crystal ashtray with twenty odd butt ends inside. She only socially smoked at dinner parties and balls, but now it looked like she'd taken up a new habit— something to comfort her during this difficult time.

The phrase 'difficult time' is an understatement when your daughter is abducted, thought Alberto, when he saw the state that his wife was in. He never felt so grim.

The fireplace was never lit, but it was certainly a cosy area—one that Veronica often used when drinking and in need of some alone time.

Alberto removed his shoes and slipped into a pair of comfortable slippers before making his way to where his wife was seated, gulping down her drink.

'Where's the parcel?' he asked bluntly, his face pale and anxious.

Veronica signalled towards the other side of the room to the side table by the minibar, where many utility bills were stacked up in a neat pile next to the house phone. With a trembling hand, she drowsily downed her vodka-tonic and he could tell it wasn't her first drink of the day. Any other day he would have told her that she'd had enough. But not today—whatever comforted her (twenty cigarettes included).

The truth was, he felt weak and hopeless. And although he wouldn't admit it—including to Veronica—he blamed himself for Daniela's kidnapping. He should have kept her closer to home. It could be argued that even though most students go to university away from home, Daniela wasn't like most students. Alberto knew that there could be people out there that would do anything to ruin him because of his position as Ambassador.

He carefully examined the parcel. It was a standard brown envelope, one that could be purchased from any post office or stationary shop. He gave it a slight squeeze and felt bubble wrap inside. The address was written in sloppy handwriting. Just about readable, but not so bad that it would get rejected. The letter C was stamped on the side with green ink, indicating that like all parcels sent to the Flores residence, it had been checked by the embassy security beforehand.

Bracing himself, Alberto took a deep breath as he carefully tore open the parcel. Veronica stood up and strolled towards him, her long silky dress dancing with her every stride. Standing beside him, she eagerly eyed the package, curious about what was inside and what information it would give (if any) about her daughter.

My poor angel, she thought, trying hard not to lose her mind, but she could feel herself doing so.

Alberto peered into the darkness of the parcel and carefully slid his hand inside. He felt a piece of paper shuffling against his palm, and then at the bottom of the package, he felt the tips of his fingers pushing against something soft but also bony. It felt like a pen with a rubbery body and yet it also felt like something awkwardly familiar. Impatiently, he grabbed it and pulled it out from the parcel.

For a second or two, both he and Veronica stared blankly at the amputated finger in disbelief. It was thin, pale, and stained in dirt and blood. Dark-red flesh dangled from the bottom, where it had been cut. When Veronica finally registered what she was looking at, she let out a scream so loud that Alberto dropped the finger on the ground. It bounced, changed direction, and then bounced off Alberto's shin like a bouncy ball. Veronica followed as she also hit the ground. Alberto stood in shock for a very long time without flinching and stared at the finger and his unconscious wife both lying on the floor before him.

27

RICARDO had been watching the warehouse for a couple of hours. It was in a secluded scrapyard a mile or two away from Dover. He hid some distance away, watching the place with a pair of night-vision binoculars while leaning against the side of a large bin container. So far, he had counted two kidnappers—a tall skinny man who was the driver who had kidnapped Daniela, and a petite girl who was a chain-smoker. Neither of them looked like they could be the mastermind behind this horrendous crime that had shaken most of the country—and even Mexico. For a start, they were too young, and secondly, the man kept coming outside to make the occasional call like he was receiving instructions from someone.

It was getting late. Ricardo waited for the right moment to rescue Daniela. He didn't call the police. It wasn't because he didn't trust them—although if he was frank, he had his doubts about trusting them. But the truth of it was that this would be his victory—his time to shine, and he would be honoured by his country and become a true hero.

Notifying the police would mean that they would get all the glory—and *he* wouldn't be remembered—even though he was the one who found Daniela. He could sense that something was wrong when he saw the Embassy car pulling up outside Daniela's maisonette. And thanks to Daniela sneaking out (without him noticing) and returning late, the taxi that he ordered had plenty of time to arrive. He then got into it and the taxi followed the imposing Embassy car from some distance away to avoid detection.

He could have sworn he heard a female voice screaming from inside the warehouse. It was high-pitched and full of fear. The adrenalin ran fast through his veins as he waited, praying that both the kidnappers would leave Daniela unattended at some point. Ten minutes was all he needed to go down there and rescue her. He was sure he could take on the man. He was taller than Ricardo, but lanky and lacking in muscle. He couldn't have been any older than nineteen, and was probably inexperienced at fighting compared to Ricardo, who was an expert at Jiu-Jitsu, Tae Kwon Do and Muay Thai.

At six minutes past midnight, the opportunity finally presented itself. The young man stepped outside the warehouse and walked towards a small plastic cabin at the other end of the yard, which appeared to be an office of some kind. Ricardo watched through the night-vision binoculars and focused on a desk with stationery and files through a window. The man walked past the desk and disappeared into another room. Then, a couple of seconds later, the lights went out. The petite girl went around the other side of the warehouse, sat on a wooden box with the words Tropical Bananas printed on, and faced the scrapyard entrance, while lighting another cigarette and fiddling on her phone. Ricardo realised that they were taking turns to keep guard while the other slept.

Silently, he crept to the rear fence close to the warehouse and waited for a moment, while scanning the area around him. The place vaguely smelled of burnt rubber. He listened carefully for any footsteps—especially those of the girl, who was just at the other side, no further than twenty metres away. But there was nothing but an eerie silence. Even the dog, which had been barking for a while some distance away, had melted away into the night.

Ricardo scanned the fence looking for any gaps to slide through, but it was all nicely sealed. He then looked up, examining the height of the fence. Luckily, it wasn't barbed at the top—but it was about five metres high. The dog up the hill started barking again, this time more aggressively as if it was trying to warn about him trespassing—which was fine, as it would undoubtedly drown out any noise that he was making.

After slowly making it to the top, he carefully put his leg over as he tightly held onto the metal gaps, which he was sure had created an indent of diamond patterns on his palm's skin. He then pulled himself over and slowly started to climb down. There was intense pain in his arms and palms that made him want to take the leap, but he decided that it was still too high up, and if he ended up getting hurt from the fall, he could be taken hostage himself—or even worse. Therefore, he climbed further down and when he was sure he was close enough, he jumped—maybe still too soon for safety. His hands and arms had started to feel numb, so he didn't care about the height any more. He rolled on the floor—putting his arms over his head to protect himself. He stumbled as he tried to get up. His left ankle felt sprained, and there was pain in his elbows and hands to the point of numbness.

The metal building was almost the same length as a football pitch. Hobbling up to the door, he carefully slid it open, which made a slight squeaking sound, and entered into the darkness.

Inside, Daniela felt lightheaded and started to lose focus. Neither the driver nor Julie had been to check on her for a while. Although she needed water, she refused to drink the bowl they had filled up for her—she couldn't remember her mouth ever being this dry. She should have been hungry too, but had no appetite.

Ron had stopped moaning and twitching a while ago and this scared her. She'd never seen anyone die before or even a dead body for that matter. Her eyes had been accustomed to the dark so she could make out the large pool of blood beneath him.

Footsteps were fast approaching, and it didn't sound like Julie or the driver. Whoever it was, they were hurriedly limping in her direction, with one foot scraping the floor.

'Let me go!' she begged hoarsely.

'HUSHH!' came a reply. 'Keep quiet!'

She saw a man approach with a black suit. When she had a clearer view, she noticed that he was of Latin origin and was almost as tall as the driver. His trousers were torn, and his shoes were muddy.

'Who're you?' she blinked.

'Keep it down! They'll hear us!' he whispered sharply. 'I'm getting you outta here!'

'Thank you!' she cried.

'Easy!' he said, gesturing for her to stay calm, as he walked behind her to examine the rope that tightly bound her wrists together.

He then removed a mini Swiss Army Knife from his back pocket, unfolded one of the metal sections that had a saw, and started to cut through the rope while she watched him carefully. He had a slight wheeze and was sweating badly.

'You still haven't told me who you are,' she said with a frown. 'How do I know that I can trust you?'

He stopped and looked at her. 'My name is Ricardo Matos. Your father hired me to keep an eye on you.'

'Well, you did a great job,' she said.

'Yeah,' he breathed as he continued to saw.

Her instinct was correct. He was the spy that her father had sent. The fact that he had located her was a surprise. She almost asked him how he had done it, but she refrained from doing so. She was scared, weak, and thirsty and just wanted to get the hell out of there. And the other two could appear at any second.

After five minutes of struggling to cut through the rope, Ricardo finally managed to set Daniela free. She slowly stood up on her numb legs and would have fallen sideward if it wasn't for him holding onto her arm. She turned and looked at Ron.

When Ricardo noticed him, he breathed something under his breath, hurried over to his prone body, and uncovered him. Daniela wept when she had a clear view. Ron lay with his eyes closed and mouth open. He was stained with blood, which had flowed out of where his little finger had been cut off.

Although Ricardo felt sure that Ron was gone, he checked for a pulse anyway. He knew that it had to be checked just in case. He had heard stories of the *dead* suddenly coming back to life, just because someone had wrongly assumed that they were *dead*.

'There's a pulse! He might make it,' he said, getting back up. 'But he'll slow us down. We need to get out of here and notify the police. It's better like that.'

Daniela wiped her tears with her sleeve, not wanting to leave Ron behind—but Ricardo was right. There was no way they could escape unseen if they tried to carry Ron out with them.

'Do you know him?' asked Ricardo as he started limping towards the entrance.

Daniela nodded. 'He's Julie's boyfriend,' she said, hurriedly following from behind.

'Whose boyfriend?' asked Ricardo, turning and giving her an odd look.

'Mine!' came a voice from the darkness ahead.

Both Ricardo and Daniela froze as Julie materialised in front of them. She had that crazy look in her eye that Daniela had seen many times before, but this time it was different. She looked mad—although she didn't appear to be surprised that Ricardo had set Daniela free—she did look profoundly agitated.

'JULIE, GET OUT THE WAY!' cried Daniela.

'Neither of you are goin' anywhere!' she replied coldly. 'What do you think this is? A game?'

Ricardo puffed out his cheeks, grabbed Daniela by the arm, and pulled her along. With an unconcerned expression on her face, Julie just stood in front of the warehouse door with her arms crossed as she watched them charging towards her.

A sudden loud bang echoed through the building, causing Daniela to stumble backward. She then realised that it wasn't the bang that caused her to fall back, but Ricardo's grip tightening on her arm as he fell. Eventually, he let go and was on the floor next to her, his hands over his chest as blood poured through his fingers.

It took Daniela a minute to realise what was happening as the driver emerged from behind Julie, holding a pistol. Suddenly, Ricardo exhaled a large gush of air as his hands fell to his sides and hit the ground—his eyes remained open, staring in sorrow at Daniela as she screamed.

'NOOOOO!!!'

'It'll be your turn next, if you don't shut the fuck up!' Julie spat at her as she walked up and pulled her from the floor by her hair.

'I wouldn't do anything without the MP's permission!' said the driver. 'Now go tie her up again!'

'Three bags full, Sir!' Julie answered sarcastically.

'Julie! Who's the MP?' whispered Daniela when she started tying her up to the same place as before.

Julie kneeled, so she was at her level, and looked deep into Daniela's eyes.

'Oh, that's right. You don't know. You'll find out soon enough' she said, seductively playing with Daniela's hair.

She then moved her hand and lightly stroked her cheek. Daniela froze in shock, not responding.

'I can see what all the fuss is about you,' she added with a wink as she stood up. 'Sweet dreams …well, at least try to.'

She then walked away, giving Ricardo's lifeless body a hard kick on the way out.

28

THE police station was one big circus with new faces racing around, as well as the regular ones rushing up and down the corridors. The security in the city was at an all-time high. Kean arranged to meet O'Leary and Pamela at the forensics department. On the way, he bumped into Noel.

'Inspector, I see you managed to crawl your way back into the case,' he said, giving Kean a patronising smile.

'I don't think I had much choice. Suddenly everyone seems to be involved,' replied Kean looking around the crowded corridor.

'That is true. But I don't want you forgetting who's still in charge.'

'Could I ever,' Kean mumbled under his breath.

'I heard that the Ambassador has stepped down.'

'Really?'

'Yes, about an hour ago,' said Noel checking his watch. 'I guess the kidnapper really has him by the balls, huh?'

'That's one way of putting it,' said Kean, trying to get past Noel.

'Where're you going?'

'Just lay off me, Noel! You're not *my* boss.'

'You know ...why don't you go home and get some rest?'

Kean raised a smile. 'I get the impression that you don't want me here.'

'What gives you that idea?'

Kean was just about to answer when Noel's phone rang. It was the perfect opportunity to leave. He hurried towards the stairs and headed down to forensics. He took a swift glance behind and noticed Noel had his back turned and was in deep conversation with whoever had called him.

'I know! Mexico is expected to make an official statement about his resignation soon!' his voice was echoing from the other side of the glass door.

When Kean walked into the forensics lab, Pamela and O'Leary were standing over a monitor, examining some data with mugs of coffee in their hands.

'Inspector, we have a perfect match on who it was that typed the suicide note!' said Pamela excitedly.

'And the answer is—'

'It was, in fact, Julie West.'

'She also sent an email to her uncle from Ron's library user account asking for money …so a perfect match was made by comparing both algorithms,' explained O'Leary.

'The typing pattern also indicated that the dominant hand was the left. And guess what! Saleem was killed by a left-handed person,' added Pamela.

'This is sufficient evidence! Let's pay Miss West a visit!' said Kean.

O'Leary and Pamela shot each other an uncomfortable look.

'Noel sent Sergeant Roberts and Barnes out earlier. Both Julie West and Ron Blates haven't been seen for a couple of days. The landlord assumes they've done a runner without paying the rent. There's an ongoing search for them,' explained O'Leary.

'They need to be tracked down fast. Especially Julie!' sighed Kean.

'Actually, Inspector, we might already have another lead.'

Pamela walking over to her desk, produced a shaded piece of paper with white squiggles on it and handed it over to Kean.

'The electrostatic detection device showed a name and a phone number. It must have been written on a piece of paper on top of the ransom note that was sent to the Ambassador.'

'I had the number checked out, and it belongs to a Richard Barker. The name and number are registered to an address in Tilmanstone,' added O'Leary.

Kean focused on the sloppy handwriting which read: *Richard*, followed by the phone number.

'Let's go!' he said, storming out of the room with O'Leary following him.

'You're welcome!' Pamela called after them. 'Pam saves the day once again, but does she get any *thanks*? Nope!'

The farmhouse in Tilmanstone, which was eight miles north of Dover, was an ancient building, possibly dating back to the eleventh century. It had stables beside it, surrounded by green orchard fields, and was about a mile from the main road.

'A perfect place to retire,' said O'Leary getting out of the car and observing the fields nearby.

'I'm not thinking about retiring just yet, O'Leary,' replied Kean with a slight smile.

As they cautiously approached the farmhouse, the horses in the stables next door sounded restless.

'Be careful, Inspector. I don't have a good feeling about this,' whispered O'Leary, shadowing Kean from behind.

'There must be a rational explanation. It just doesn't make sense. The guy's seventy-two with no criminal record,' said Kean as he reached for the doorbell.

A couple of seconds later, an elderly lady answered the door and gave a bewildered look when she saw them.

'Yes, how can I help you?' she asked, wincing at Kean, who was standing closer to the door.

'I'm Inspector Nicolas Kean, and this is Sergeant O'Leary. We're looking for a Mr Richard Barker,' said Kean flashing his badge at her.

'Oh, I see. Just hang on,' she said, her brows crossing with concern. She then disappeared inside.

Shortly after, an elderly man materialised at the door. He was thin and had a bony face with white stubble and a crooked nose (like it had taken a beating sometime throughout his life). He had small bright blue eyes, which curiously looked at O'Leary and then at Kean.

'How can I help you officers?' he asked politely.

'Mr Richard Barker, we're investigating a crime and your name and phone number were found on a piece of evidence,' explained Kean.

'We were wondering if you could enlighten us on how it got there,' added O'Leary bluntly.

Barker stared at them with a puzzled look. 'My name and phone number on a piece of evidence? You better come in. It's cold outside,' he told them.

They followed him into the living room, which had pale pink wallpaper and old black and white pictures in frames of the couple in their younger years. His wife, Ruth Barker, asked them if they wanted tea. They thanked her and declined. Being offered anything to drink had always been against the rules, even if it was a glass of water. Especially if it was offered by suspects. Kean felt the adrenalin rushing through his veins when it occurred to him that Daniela could be close by.

'The forensics team has used an electrostatic detection device on a ransom letter. It turns out that someone wrote your name and number on a sheet of paper which was on top of the one on which the ransom note was written,' explained Kean.

Barker fell silent for a moment as the information sank in.

'I have no idea how it got there,' he then chuckled nervously.

'Whoever wrote this is responsible for multiple murders and the kidnapping of the Mexican Ambassador's daughter. Mr Barker, I hope you can help us.'

'You mean *The Silent Killer?*' he whispered with a shaky voice.

Kean nodded, then took out a copy of the paper with his name and phone number and handed it over to him. 'Do you recognise the handwriting? Whoever wrote this must know you.'

Barker studied the paper, then shook his head, exhaling some air as his eyes widened with anger. 'That fucking piece of shit!' he gasped.

With a huff, he stood up and limped out of the room. O'Leary was about to follow him, but Kean indicated for him to remain seated. The man could barely walk, never mind outrun them. After a minute or two, he returned holding another piece of paper, which he handed over to Kean. When O'Leary saw the astonished look on Kean's face, this time he did get up and walked over to him. When he saw what was on the paper, O'Leary was just as startled as Kean. It was the original piece of paper with Richard Barker's name and number on it.

'Who wrote this!?' screeched Kean.

'Jamie Sturridge. A young lad who looks after the grounds and the stables from time to time.'

Kean turned and looked at O'Leary, who was jotting down the name.

'Where is he?'

'He said he was going away for a while. When my wife and I went to Cardiff to visit my sister-in-law, Jamie looked after the stables. When I was there, I lost my phone. So, I got myself a new number. That's when he must have written it down.'

'Did he say where he was going away to?' asked Kean.

'I think he said he was going to Birmingham. But then he said he didn't know and was quite vague about it.'

Kean and O'Leary gave each other a look.

'Did he mention why he was going?' asked O'Leary hesitantly.

Barker shook his head. 'Nope, he just said he was going.'

'And you haven't seen him since?'

'Not that I can recall.'

'Where does Jamie Sturridge live?'

'He lives with his mum just down the road from here.'

O'Leary jotted down the address, they thanked Barker for his time, and left.

The house was in a council estate with a dozen children on the road riding their dilapidated bikes, and others running around chasing each other. Some stopped and gawked as the police car drove past—while others ran and hid in their houses. O'Leary parked right outside Sturridge's house. The lawn was a mess with broken toys, a rusty swing, and a dirty old thrown out bathtub.

'The place is a slum,' mumbled O'Leary as he turned off the engine and stepped out of the car.

Kean pressed on the doorbell, but it didn't ring, so instead he gave a couple of firm knocks on the door. A plump lady with short black hair answered. She was dressed in a pink tracksuit top with clashing red tracksuit bottoms and must have had the biggest gold earrings Kean had ever seen. When he looked down, he noticed she was barefoot, her toes had blue nail varnish, and her feet were dirty like she hadn't washed in a very long time.

The smell of fried oil hit them hard.

'We're with the South-East Police Department,' Kean said, flashing his badge. 'We're looking for James Sturridge.'

'Is he in trouble?'

'We just need to talk to him,' replied Kean.

The lady grinned and said, 'Jamie's away on business. I 'aven't seen him in weeks.'

'What business is he away on?' O'Leary asked.

The lady looked left and then right as if she was about to cross the road and leaned closer to them. 'He's a secret agent you see,' she whispered with a wink. 'But promise you won't tell anyone!'

'We promise,' said Kean, sensing O'Leary roll his eyes next to him.

A little girl with ginger hair and two side ponytails appeared from behind and snuggled up to her.

'Are you a real policeman?' she asked O'Leary, who was in uniform.

'Hello, young lady. We are indeed,' he smiled.

'My foster child,' said the lady, putting an arm around the little girl.

'What's your name?' Kean asked the girl with a grin.

'Lisa,' she answered.

'That's a beautiful name. How old are you, Lisa?'

'I'm five,' she said.

'You're a big girl, aren't you?'

Lisa nodded with a cheeky smile, showing her missing front teeth.

Kean looked up at the lady. 'And how about Jamie? What's his relation to you?'

'He's my son.'

'Why did you say he's a secret agent? Did he tell you that?'

She nodded.

'Do you know where we can find him?' asked O'Leary.

'No, he didn't tell me where he was going. But they never do!' she winked.

'Do you know why he went?' tried Kean.

'No idea,' she said and stopped for a moment. 'Actually, he might 'ave mentioned something about helping out some Mexican politician, but my memory isn't what it used to be, you know.'

Kean's heart started to race. 'Did he say what the Mexican politician's name was?' he asked impatiently.

She shook her head. 'Sorry, he didn't.'

'Can we have Jamie's number?'

'You can, but it's been disconnected.'

Kean looked at O'Leary, who shot a disappointed glance back at him.

'If you do find him, tell him to give his mother a call, the little shit!' she exclaimed with a chuckle.

'Will do,' replied Kean. 'Do you have a recent photo of Jamie?'

'I should have. Wait 'ere,' she said and went inside to retrieve one. Not long after, she returned with a photo.

'I found this one, but it's 'bout two years old,' she said, passing it over to Kean.

Kean examined the picture. Jamie had short black hair, grey frowning eyes, and was wearing an earring. 'That will do,' he said. 'Can we borrow it?'

The lady thought for a moment, then replied, 'Sure!'

29

INSPECTOR Kean pulled up at the Harborne Police station in Birmingham just as Pamela called. He answered, letting the call go through to the car's speaker.

'Are you in your office, Inspector?' she asked.

'No, I'm in Birmingham. Saleem's mother finally decided to talk. How can I help you?'

'The forensic unit in London have confirmed that the amputated finger does not belong to Daniela.'

'At least that's good news, right? So, whose is it?'

'It's the little finger of a male between the age of 17 and 20. That's all the information we have.'

Kean fell silent, wondering who the finger could belong to—then a number of other questions followed: *Was there another hostage? How were Julie and Ron involved? Were they working together or for someone else?*

He was missing something. Something he couldn't quite put his finger on. Any other day he would have laughed at the *finger* pun, but not today. Jamie, Ron and Julie seemed the most unlikely of friends. They were worlds apart. But something—or someone—brought them all together as part of the same criminal organisation.

"After hanging up, Kean got out of the car and entered the station where he was greeted by Sandra Ricks, who worked for the Protected Persons Service. She had a friendly smile and seemed too nice to be working for this particular department. She was in her early sixties and looked more like a primary school teacher.

'We've been hiding her in a secret location,' said Sandra softly. 'After her brother was murdered, she started getting paranoid that she'd be next.'

'How come she agreed to talk all of a sudden?' asked Kean, as he followed Sandra into another corridor and down some stairs where it as darker with dimmed lights.

Sandra turned and met Kean's eyes.

'She seems less afraid since the murder of her son. Seems to care less. We're taking extra precautions as the psychiatrist report states that she could be suicidal.'

'Not surprising after everything she's gone through,' said Kean.

They arrived at a door at the end of the corridor with a policeman standing guard. He told them to write their names and the time on a register before unlocking the door for them to enter. The room was dark—even darker than the corridor—and it took the Inspector a while to get used to the dimness. At the far end sat a lady with a headscarf. She looked like she was in her seventies.

'Awja, this is Inspector Nicolas Kean. He's investigating your son's murder,' Sandra explained.

Awja nodded, without looking up at them.

Sandra turned to Kean and nodded.

Kean slowly walked up to Awja who still avoided eye contact—without a flinch, she just sat with her hands cupped together, staring towards the door.

'I'm sorry about the death of your son—'

'My son, Saleem, was a good kid!' she cut in with a hoarse voice. 'And let me tell you something. He loved that girl very much!'

Kean looked back at Sandra, who shrugged dismissively.

'But she didn't know him. And to be honest, he didn't really know her either,' he said, casting his attention back to Awja.

Awja suddenly looked at Kean, making full eye contact for the first time. 'Love is spiritual. Why did they need to know each other at all?'

Kean considered what she had said but couldn't give her an answer. Her glare was so intense that it made him feel uncomfortable—almost hypnotised to the extent that he could hardly move.

'I don't expect you to understand. But you should know that my dear son Saleem was used!'

'Who was he used by? I need a name!' urged Kean, who now seemed to be the one avoiding eye contact.

'They had promised him he would be together with her. But now, instead, he is *dead*!' she suddenly broke down and began to cry, covering her face with her bony hands.

Kean moved closer to her and spoke more softly this time. 'Who was it that promised him? Was it the same person who helped him escape from Oakwood?'

She was hesitant for a moment, unsure whether she should answer. But eventually she did.

'Yes. And they killed my brother too! They also used him!' she explained, wiping her teary eyes with the palms of her hands.

'Please, give me a name!' Kean tried again.

'I have no idea,' she said disappointedly.

Now that his eyes had become accustomed to the dimness of the room, he noticed that her face was full of wrinkles and a couple of scars. Sometimes, it is not necessary to guess whether someone has suffered a tough or violent life. And Awja certainly fit that category.

'But I know he's from Mexico,' she said.

Kean's eyes widened. 'Did you ever see him?'

She slowly shook her head.

'My brother Usman did. And now he's dead. I do not want to be in that category. You are looking for someone who calls themselves the *Mexican Politician*. What I do know is that they are manipulative, charming …and very violent.'

Kean looked back at Sandra. She was now busy taking notes with a worried look.

He thanked Awja Raza for her time, and also thanked Sandra, then got into his car and started making his way back south towards Canterbury. He couldn't help but think that being a politician himself, Alberto must have been involved somehow. Even if he wasn't, he must have known the killer. Or was the killer claiming to be a Mexican politician to put the police off track? After all, like Awja had said, he was manipulative. Kean was now certain of one thing—Julie, Ron and Jamie were working for the Mexican Politician, who the media had nicknamed *The Silent Killer*.

Viola was sitting patiently waiting in Room 2 when Sergeant O'Leary walked in. He noticed she looked pale with teary eyes that had red rings around them. He placed himself opposite her and tried to raise a friendly smile— something he was forced to do from time to time.

'Thank you for coming quickly at such short notice,' he said.

She nervously nodded, noticing something in his hand. It was a photo.

'I want you to tell me if this is the driver whose car Daniela got into,' he added, sliding the photo over to her.

At first, she hesitated, then slowly picked it up—unsure whether she wanted to look at it and see his rotten face again. She took a deep breath, turned it over and examined the picture of Jamie Sturridge, her eyes widening as she brought it up closer to her face.

'*Bastardo!*' she breathed under her breath.

A single tear slid down her cheek. Involuntarily, she let go of the photo as it slipped off the table top and onto to the floor.

'Is that the man who drove Daniela Flores?' asked O'Leary. Although he knew the answer from her reaction, he needed her to say it for the recording.

She nodded and sniffed. 'Yes.'

'Thank you for your time,' he said.

She nodded again.

'By the way, does Alberto Flores have any enemies who are Mexican? Anyone who'd want to kidnap Daniela?'

Viola thought for a moment, then shook her head.

'Not to my knowledge. But then again, what do I know? I'm just a maid. I'm not involved in the politics.'

'I understand,' replied O'Leary. 'You have my number if you hear or think of anything else that might help us.'

'Can I go now? I feel claustrophobic,' said Viola.

O'Leary nodded, and Viola quickly got up and went for the door, covering her mouth with one hand, trying to prevent herself from throwing up in front of O'Leary. When she was out of the room, he could hear her coughing and gagging echoing in the corridor.

O'Leary waited for a moment for the place to become silent and made a call to Kean.

'Inspector, the maid has just confirmed that Jamie Sturridge *is* the driver.'

30

INSPECTOR Noel Griffiths looked up with irritation as Kean entered the room during his meeting with the sergeants. He hesitated for a second, then continued talking.

Locating an empty seat in the cramped meeting room, Kean made himself comfortable while studying the writing and the diagrams that were splattered all over the whiteboard behind Griffiths.

'At the end of the day, we're dealing with a small gang of young people who're trying to get money from Alberto Flores by threatening to keep his daughter hostage. We know that they were initially a gang of four. James Sturridge, Julie West, Ron Banks, and Saleem Raza. But Raza was murdered by the others for an obvious reason—'

'An *obvious* reason?' called out Kean.

Everyone turned and looked at him. There were a couple of chuckles from some of the sergeants around the room.

Noel frowned at him. 'That's right. An *obvious* reason,' he muttered uncomfortably.

'I'm sorry,' said Kean. 'It's just not too obvious for me. Can you please clarify?'

'Is it not, Inspector Kean?' Noel managed to raise an uncomfortable smile. 'James, Julie, and Ron decided to get rid of Saleem when they found out that Rash wasn't his true name. They panicked thinking he was some kind of spy.'

'That's very dramatic, but it doesn't make sense. This group of young people are being manipulated. They are all being used by someone who wants to destroy Alberto Flores!'

'You watch too many gangster movies, Nick!' laughed Noel. 'There is no one else involved except this small gang of students. And if you ask me, the others who were killed were also gang members! And when they killed them, their share of the ransom money increased!'

'Now, that's not fair to ruin the reputation of these kids that were murdered! It's not fair on them—or their parents!'

'Oh, wake up, Inspector! These kids are not innocent victims! No one's getting *manipulated*. They are a dangerous gang that should be caught as soon as possible. And the ones who died were also gang members! No question about it!'

'Listen, there's some Mexican politician who is manipulating Julie West, Jamie Sturridge, Ron Banks, and Saleem Raza—before he was killed—in order to ruin Alberto Flores by killing whoever got close to Daniela and eventually kidnapping her!'

'You're mad! That is a scandalous accusation! One that will ruin our relationship with Mexico,' laughed Noel. 'Victor Silva and Harry Barnes were also in the gang, and that's that! As for Jose, he tripped and fell off the edge of the wall.'

'What evidence do you have?'

'I'm not going to discuss anything further with you, Inspector Kean! You have already disrupted this meeting. Go home! Get some rest! You look like you need it.'

Kean looked around the room—everyone avoided eye contact. Some subtly shook their heads with disappointment at Noel's attitude, or maybe it was the way he was approaching the case.

'Fine …I'll go,' Kean said eventually. 'But just a friendly bit of advice—don't ruin the reputation of those victims.'

Noel sighed with a mocking smile as his eyes followed Kean out the room.

When Kean entered his office, his phone was ringing, so he hurried towards it and picked it up. It was Constable Reading from the front desk. He notified him that he had a visitor. Kean rarely had any visitors, so he was taken aback and asked who it was. When Reading told him who it was, it was an even bigger surprise.

'Alberto Flores?' repeated Kean.

'Shall I send him through, Inspector?' asked Reading.

'Yes, send him to my office.'

Multiple thoughts rushed through the Inspector's mind. As Alberto wanted to see him personally, he must have been aware of his relationship with Daniela. Or did he just want to check in on the investigation? He suddenly started feeling very guilty. It wasn't long until there was a knock on the door. And even before Kean had a chance to answer, Alberto walked straight in. Kean was amazed at how cool and composed he looked. In no way did he seem like a man whose daughter was missing.

'At last, we meet Inspector Kean,' he said, shutting the door behind him.

'Indeed. Please take a seat.'

Although he was no longer the Ambassador, Alberto still appeared authoritative in his navy-blue suit and tie. He walked up to Kean's desk as if he owned the office. He had a neat haircut, was freshly shaven, and certainly didn't look like he was going through such a difficult time as Kean had imagined. Placing himself on the chair opposite, he shot Kean a sincere look.

'I hear you were close to my daughter,' he said candidly.

Kean froze for a second—he felt his heart race.

'How can I help you, Mr Flores?'

Alberto's reaction shocked him. He sensed his desperation piercing through from what he said next—and even felt sorry for the man.

'You must know something. She must have mentioned *something* to you!'

'Actually, I was hoping maybe you could shed some light on the matter.'

Now it was Alberto's turn to look confused.

'What do you mean?'

'The kidnappers have been bragging that they are working for a Mexican politician. Maybe a rival of yours?'

Alberto looked dumbfoundedly at Kean.

'Just doesn't make sense. All these murders seem like the work of a serial killer. I can't think of anyone who would go to such great lengths to do something like this.'

Kean noticed Alberto's eyes examining the board behind him with the pinned photos of the victims, scattered with post-it notes which were all related to the case.

'The person we are looking for is pure evil. They are manipulative and so discrete that even the court will have trouble pinning the crime on them. We're searching for someone who not only forced you to resign from your position as Ambassador, but has taken your most precious thing.'

Alberto felt cold sweat trickling down his forehead as he undid his top button and loosened his tie.

'If you can think of anyone—'

'I'll call you,' he cut in. 'I'm staying at the Westgate Hotel.'

'Not in the house you rented for Daniela?'

'No, I can't stay there,' he shook his head, his eyes turning red and watery. The waiting is the worst part …the uncertainty. I'd happily pay the money now to get her back. As long as my angel is safe!'

'I know,' is all Kean could think to say.

31

AFTER Jamie wrapped a bin bag around Ricardo's body and dragged it to the dumpster, he sat on one of the wooden boxes outside the warehouse and lit a cigarette. Ricardo's eyes started to haunt him. They remained open with an expression of shock, staring back at him with a cold gaze, even after he was dead. So, Jamie first covered his head then his muscular body with a bin bag—which was even heavier than it appeared. This made dragging the body to the dumpster a challenge.

That bitch, Julie, didn't even help. In theory, I should now get paid more than her because I killed someone to save the fucking mission, he thought. *I wonder if the MP will consider it—plus the psychological damage that killing someone might have caused me.*

Jamie felt his hand shaking uncontrollably as he anxiously took a massive puff of his roll-up. He tried hard to keep it together while asking himself how he had become a murderer. He guessed that no one planned to become one. It just happens. Ask any small child what they want to be when they grow up, and they will either say a pilot, fireman, or a doctor—but never an assassin.

...but I'm not a murderer. Murderers are evil. Look at James Bond, killing for the greater good to save the day—and this is precisely what I have done, he kept assuring himself.

As far as he was concerned, he was fighting to stabilise the United Kingdom's relationship with Mexico. The Mexican Politician had convinced him that he was on the side of good. Jamie felt sorry for Daniela, as she was innocent in all this, but she couldn't help having an evil father.

Julie walked past him.

'Nice work, arsehole!' she sighed sharply as she made her way to the cabin where the office was, but Jamie ignored her as his mind wandered to when he had first met with MP, who told him he was some politician from Mexico.

It was a dull day—like many others at that time—grey clouds covered the sky, as Jamie hurried to do some cleaning at the Barker stables before it started to rain. That's when a black car had pulled up next to him as he raced down the sidewalk. The driver's window wound down, and there was a tanned man with slicked-back hair, sitting behind the wheel.

'I hear you do the odd job, kid,' he called at him, as drops of rain started to fall from the sky.

'And who the fuck are you?' was Jamie's response as he walked faster.

'You want to make some extra cash?'

Jamie looked left and then right. The street was deserted. He stopped and turned to face the man.

'Call me racist, but I don't work for foreigners,' he said bluntly.

The man didn't seem fazed by Jamie's comment and produced a stack of fifties from his blazer's inner pocket.

'Even if it's going to make you rich?' he said, with a Cheshire Cat grin.

Now Jamie was the one who was fazed. Coming from a poor background, he had never seen a stack of cash that was as thick as a brick.

'There's more, but you have to work for it,' added the man, handing the cash to Jamie.

'Sure. Why not? I'll work,' he said softly. 'What do you want me to do?'

'I'm renting the old warehouse down the road. There's some cleaning to be done.'

'What? The one in the scrapyard? Yeah alright. I was just on my way to clean some stables, but I'll cancel,' said Jamie transfixed on the cash he was holding.

'No, you won't! Go and finish your work at the stables first, and don't tell anyone about the warehouse! No one must know!'

Jamie, a little confused, nodded, 'Alright.'

'And put that away!'

'Sorry,' said Jamie, shoving the thick stack of notes into the large pocket of his old painter's trousers and buttoning it up.

Later, when he'd finished at the stables, soaking wet from the rain, he hurried to the scrapyard where the old warehouse was. The man in the suit was waiting for him, standing next to his car, and Jamie noticed that he was almost as tall as him.

'I knew I could count on you,' said the man with a Latin American accent.

'So, where shall I start cleaning?' asked Jamie.

'Jamie, Jamie, Jamie, you won't be doing any cleaning,' chuckled the man.

'What do you mean? And how the fuck do you know my name?'

'You think you get that much payment just for cleaning an old scrapyard? The truth is, you'll be doing some spy work. You'll help your country get out of a political mess by strengthening ties with Mexico!'

Jamie was silent for a moment. He stared at him wide-eyed. He had no idea what the man was talking about, and to be honest, he didn't give a *flying shit*—he remembered thinking at the time. All he knew was that he was going to get rich.

'You mean I will be a spy?'

'That's right! But you can't tell anyone!' the man had warned.

Jamie smiled. 'So, you're from Mexico.'

'See!? You're smarter than I thought! Got the makings of a perfect spy,' the man smiled back.

'What's your name?'

'You can call me MP. It's short for Mexican Politician,'

Jamie didn't dare question what his real name was.

MP explained that his first assignment would be a trip to Birmingham to help a doctor and an IT technician to assist a victim to escape from an institute. All he had to do was to drive them to a secure location. He did stop and wonder if it was legal—but the money was too good for him to *give a fuck*. Plus, he strongly wanted to believe that he had become a spy.

Julie came rushing back out with her mobile tightly clenched in her hand, bringing Jamie back to the present.

She marched up to him and said, 'Just spoke to MP. You need to unwrap the body!'

'Why?' asked Jamie, disturbed by her demanding attitude, as well has MP's request.

'Looks like we'll be posting another finger,' she smiled sadistically.

Jamie exhaled sharply. At least he didn't have to uncover the head for that, he thought, feeling slightly relieved—then the image of Ricardo's eyes crawled back into his mind, and this time they even blinked at him.

'What are you fucking waiting for!? Do it now, you mug!' blasted Julie.

32

LIKE most late mornings since her daughter's disappearance, Veronica lay in bed—not wanting to get up—feeling nauseous and sorry for herself. Huffing and cursing, she turned over to her side when the doorbell rang. She didn't want to see anyone. She felt like a fool thinking about all the times she thought she was depressed in the past, even though she wasn't. Because this was how true depression felt like—the way she was feeling now! She hated everyone. She hated her husband and despised herself even more.

The doorbell rang again, followed by a couple of hard knocks. Suddenly, her eyes opened wide as a glimmer of hope rushed through her.

'Daniela?' she exhaled sharply, pushing herself out of bed, slipping into her silk dressing gown and tying its belt around her thin waist.

The doorbell just kept ringing.

'Wait! I'm coming, darling!' she said with a broken voice—her words barely coming out.

Almost tumbling down the stairs, she rushed through the living room, up to the front door and opened it, almost giving Juan a tight hug as she thought he was Daniela standing on the doorstep. When she realised it wasn't her, Veronica slumped on the doorframe—slid to the ground—and started sobbing loudly.

'Veronica!?' called Juan, helping her back up and escorting her onto the couch next to the fireplace.

'I'm sorry,' she breathed, lying on her back looking faint with the back of her hand over her forehead. 'I thought it was—'

'I can imagine. You live in hope,' said Juan with a sympathetic look. 'I'll get you a glass of water.'

'No, I'm fine—' she replied, then stopped and stared at the parcel under his arm.

'I got this from the postman. We arrived at the same time.'

Veronica's heart started to race when she noticed the handwriting on the parcel was the same as the one used to write the ransom note that accompanied the amputated finger.

'Oh God!' she trembled, her face turning pale—her hand that had been over her forehead now covering her mouth—as if she was going to be sick.

'What is it?' Juan asked.

'The postman!'

'What about him?'

'Packages are usually checked by the embassy security first. He brought the parcel directly here! The postman must be the one who has Daniela!'

'That's ridiculous. You're being paranoid. He seemed like an official postman to me,' replied Juan dismissively. 'Plus, Alberto resigned as Ambassador, remember?'

Veronica stopped for a moment.

'I suppose you're right,' she said in a quiet voice, looking unconvinced.

'Where's my brother?' asked Juan.

'He should be here soon. He started spending most of his time in Canterbury.'

Juan held up the parcel. 'Shall I open it?'

'No!' replied Veronica hastily. 'No, thank you. It's best if Alberto opens it. He prefers it that way,' she added softly, realising that she may have overreacted at first.

'Very well,' said Juan placing it down. 'In that case, I wouldn't mind a coffee. I'll help myself. Would you like one?'

'Black. No sugar,' replied Veronica.

'I know,' smiled Juan, heading towards the main corridor and into the kitchen, which was even bigger than the flat he had rented in Mexico after coming out of jail.

'Do you need help?' called Veronica when she noticed he had taken his time to return.

'I'll be there in a minute! You just rest,' came a reply.

When Juan eventually came back, they sat silently sipping their coffees, staring at the small package on the table.

Twenty minutes later, Alberto walked through the front door, greeted by Veronica, who gestured towards the parcel, and a sympathetic-looking Juan.

'Hello, brother,' he said, standing up.

Alberto realised what Veronica was focusing on. He hurried towards the table and picked up the parcel, then he stopped and looked up.

'Veronica, you'd better leave the room.'

'Just open the damn thing!' she replied with anger.

'Suit yourself, but last time you fainted,' he reminded her, delicately tearing the parcel and slowly reaching inside, as if handling a snake. There was a piece of paper with the same sloppy handwriting as before. Alberto read it out loud.

'Dear Mr Alberto Flores, any more monkey business and you'll never lay eyes on your daughter again! Make sure there are no police close by. When you place the 10 million pounds at the flag side of the cloister garden, you can have your daughter back.'

'Monkey business?' repeated Juan with a puzzled look.

'What does that even mean?' asked Veronica.

Alberto turned the parcel over and another finger with a silver ring on it fell to the ground. The ring had the letter R engraved on it.

'Oh God!' cried Veronica, trying hard not to look at it directly.

'Christ!' said Juan from under his breath.

This time, Alberto cold-bloodedly reached down and picked it up.

'It's Ricardo's,' he said.

'Who's that?' asked Juan.

'I asked him to keep a close eye on Daniela. I take it he followed her and got caught.'

'How do you know it's his?'

'I recognise the ring. They cut off his finger that had the ring to send me as a warning.'

Juan sighed, not knowing what to say, uncomfortable with Veronica bursting into tears next to him.

'Well, I think you now know what they mean by monkey business. He thinks I sent Ricardo to rescue Daniela.'

'Wait! You didn't send him to rescue Daniela?' asked Juan.

'No, he went to Canterbury to keep an eye out for her before she was kidnapped.'

Juan walked over to Alberto and placed a hand on his shoulder. 'If there's anything I can do for you brother, let me know.'

'Thank you. I only came to London to sort out the cash for this fucking lunatic.'

Juan looked into his eyes. 'So, you're actually going to pay him.'

'Do I have any other choice?'

Juan was silent, probably thinking what he'd do if he was in the same situation.

'They've really got you,' he sighed. 'First your ambassadorship—and then the ransom money.'

'The post won't even get checked by the security any more,' said Veronica. 'You've lost power, Alberto.'

Alberto's face turned red. Quietly, he went over to the minibar and helped himself to a glass of scotch.

33

OUTSIDE, the wind howled like a wolf causing the metallic walls of the warehouse to tremble as Daniela helplessly sat slouched on the floor—her hands tightly tied behind her back and her legs bound together. She heard footsteps—ones that she recognised well, like iron hammers banging into the ground. Julie, holding a sandwich, approached her. Daniela quickly glanced up and then looked back down at the floor.

'It's cheese and ham. My favourite,' said Julie, offering it to her with a friendly smile.

Daniela ignored her, her red, teary eyes remaining locked on the ground. Never in her life had she felt so overwhelmed—multiple emotions ran through her mind. She missed her mum and her dad, but most of all, she missed Kean. She hoped he wouldn't be stupid enough to track her down and get himself killed like Ricardo.

She felt extreme hunger and thirst, but she refused to eat or drink anything that this pair of psychos had on offer.

'You *must* eat! You need the energy for tomorrow!' Julie raised her voice, shoving the sandwich into Daniela's face.

She then noticed the bowl of water next to Daniela.

'You haven't been fucking drinking either, have you?' she said. 'I'm surprised you're still alive!'

Daniela turned away from Julie's breath, which reeked like an ashtray.

Julie let out a short, frustrated chuckle and said, 'Fine! Suit yourself!' flicking the sandwich at Daniela's face; she then marched away, calling Daniela *a fucking stubborn bitch.*

On her way out, she checked the time on her phone. It was 23:53. The MP would be here in seven minutes. It would be strange seeing him again after he'd caught the crime world by surprise, terrorising the entire country, making a name for himself as the notorious *Silent Killer.* Although he hadn't committed any of the murders directly himself, he was a true mastermind.

Outside, Jamie was sitting on one of the wooden boxes, scratching his name on its surface with his housekey. She had never understood how he could bear the freezing weather with just a worn t-shirt while she spent most of the time in the cabin, sheltered from the cold wearing her cosy puffer jacket.

'She won't fucking eat,' she told him.

'Shall we call MP?'

'No point. He'll be here any minute now.'

'How much do you think he'll pay us?' asked Jamie. Julie noticed his eyes widening with excitement.

'I dunno. But he'd better make us fucking rich!' Julie replied.

Jamie nodded and smirked at the thought of it.

As promised, the Mexican Politician arrived right at midnight. The yellow headlights of the car got brighter as it moved closer to the scrapyard through the thick fog. It then came to a sudden stop before it had completely passed through the entrance. The passenger door flung open, and a figure of a man in a long overcoat and hat materialised. He looked like something out of a black and white 1950's gangster movie.

'Nice parking,' Julie sarcastically muttered to herself.

'There it is!' said Jamie, rubbing his hands and looking at the metal briefcase that the man carried.

Julie also noticed the briefcase, but unlike Jamie, she showed little excitement.

'Just play it cool, you wanker!' she whispered at him sharply.

Irritated by her negative attitude, Jamie gave her nudge.

MP strolled up to them, wearing a friendly smile. He held the briefcase with his left hand while he had the right one tucked in his pocket.

'Hello there,' he said. 'How's our guest doing this evening? Did she have her dinner?'

Julie shook her head. 'She's refusing to eat …or drink.'

MP rested the case on the ground and clicked open its clasps.

'Well, that's a shame,' he said, opening the case and taking out a metal object—that in the darkness appeared to be a pistol.

Jamie squinted, trying to determine if it really was a gun that MP was fiddling with. But it was too dark to tell from a distance. And now it looked as if he was screwing an extra piece onto it—they assumed it was a silencer—as he slowly walked up to them.

Julie and Jamie both looked at each other, thinking the same thing—one of them would have to shoot Ron. He had fulfilled his purpose. There was no more need for him, and if she was honest with herself, Julie would feel better if he was gone. Deep inside, she felt some guilt. After all, she did use him before drugging him and cutting off his finger. It was all for the greater good, as the Mexican Politician had put it when they had first met.

He looked up and smiled after connecting the silencer to the barrel. Julie and Jamie managed to return his smile, both impatient and curious about the amount of cash that might be inside the metal case.

'Thank you both for your duties. But as I mentioned before, it's all for the greater good. So, no hard feelings,' said MP in a cold monotone voice as he raised the pistol and pointed it at Jamie, who stared back in confusion.

MP cocked his head to the side and unhesitatingly gave the trigger a sudden squeeze, causing the pistol to pop loudly. Julie let out a short yell. In shock, she glanced at Jamie, who was now cross-eyed and had a bullet hole in the middle of his forehead with blood trickling down the bridge of his nose. The dog up the hill began barking uncontrollably again as the wind inside the scrapyard started to intensify, blowing Jamie's hair in all directions—his head tilted back, and he hit the ground hard—not moving, not even a moan or a breath.

Julie started to stutter, trying to ask something to the MP, but he just ignored her muttering and pointed the pistol at her. *Pop.* She felt a dull pain on her forehead followed by a burning sensation running through her head as if her brain was on fire. She had never experienced anything so agonising—no pain was as intense as this. A sudden thought came to her, as her brain continued to swell. It was of her headmistress, Miss Winch, who had given her first ever detention at school.

'So why have you been sent to see me?' Miss Winch asked Jenifer Devlin, one of the other students, over her half-rim glasses.

'I took a shortcut during the cross-country run, Miss,' she replied.

'A Saturday afternoon's detention should teach you not to take shortcuts, Miss Devlin!'

'Yes, Miss Winch,' replied Jenifer with a sad look.

Then Miss Winch turned and faced Penny Thomas, another student, who was running with Jenifer. She'd also taken the shortcut.

'Detention!' said Winch dismissively before finally turning towards Julie.

'Miss West, what a surprise. And how come you're here?'

Julie glanced at the other girls and then back at the headmistress, contemplating whether she should be honest or just face the music. To tell the truth, she was unaware that she had even taken a shortcut. Overweight and slow, she had followed the other girls from a distance, unable to keep up. It was rainy and damp. She was tired and breathless.

'I followed them,' Julie had replied.

The headmistress nodded, but in a way that indicated she didn't believe Julie.

'Let this be a lesson in life, Julie West. Never follow the wrong people,' said Miss Winch looking deep into Julie's eyes. 'And that lesson can begin with a detention.'

In no way had that detention been a lesson for her. Otherwise, she wouldn't have followed the wrong people her entire life and ended up in this rotten scrapyard with a bullet in her head. Her last thought was of Daniela (who was perfect in every way) coming first in that cross-country run—taking no shortcuts—and how she hated her for it, but the hate did not last long, as everything swiftly went blank.

The Mexican Politician, still wearing a smirk, stepped over Julie's and Jamie's lifeless bodies and headed towards the rusty warehouse.

Daniela felt weaker than before, but hearing Julie yell outside gave her a glimmer of hope that someone had come to rescue her. She imagined it would be Kean. For the first time in her life, she realised that she truly loved someone, and her greatest fear was not seeing him again.

Footsteps echoed from the entrance at the other side of the warehouse. Daniela raised her head and focused hard, her neck stiff and her eyes burning. She felt frail and shivered uncontrollably. The figure of a man materialised, walking towards her. She noticed he had a hat, wore a long overcoat, and was holding a metal briefcase. As he approached, Daniela watched with dismay.

'How?' she asked, in disbelief.

The man gave her a friendly smile.

'Hello, mijita.'

34

'IT'S just one thing after another!' grunted Alberto in frustration, fiddling with the home security camera settings. 'All the recordings have somehow been deleted!'

'How's that possible?' asked Juan with an irritated grunt.

'Are you sure the description of the postman you gave the police was accurate?' Veronica asked him.

'How very insulting,' replied Juan somewhat dismissively.

'Finding Daniela might depend on it. So, I don't give a fuck whether you are insulted or not!'

'Wow,' Juan mocked her.

'It's no good. Won't bring up past recordings,' said Alberto, putting down the remote control.

Juan patted Alberto on the shoulder. 'Brother, I will come with you to Canterbury. I'm not letting you go alone.'

Alberto sighed. 'No, it's too risky. If you want to do something helpful, then stay here and take care of Veronica while I'm gone.'

'What do you mean by *stay here and take care of Veronica*? I'm coming with you! I cannot stay here knowing that Daniela will be in Canterbury!' gasped Veronica.

Juan stood up and walked towards the front door. 'He's right. It's too risky. I will get my stuff from the car. Hope the guest bedroom is ready!'

Veronica shot Alberto a look and shook her head disapprovingly, but before she could say anything, Alberto cut in. 'Good idea, brother. The guest bedroom *is* ready.'

Later that evening, Veronica helped Alberto with the money-counter machine. First, there was the cash that was stored in the bedroom safe—all in fifties. Although Alberto knew the amount, he didn't want to take any risks.

'Whoever it is, they must know you well enough to know that you can afford ten million,' said Veronica as she handed another bunch of notes to her husband, who made sure they were perfectly aligned before feeding them into the money-counter machine.

With a sad look, he looked up at her and removed his spectacles. 'Darling, I'm afraid there'll be some changes after we hand this over.'

'Some changes?' sighed Veronica.

Alberto looked around the room. 'We'll have to downgrade.'

Veronica's eyes turned watery. 'Albert, I don't care, as long as I get my baby back!' she sniffed.

'I know,' he said, putting his hand over hers, something he hadn't done in a long time. Ever since he'd become Ambassador, their relationship had been rocky. There was no romance. No shared feelings. With a single touch, she felt comforted and protected. But it didn't last long—Alberto sensed she was suddenly distracted when she glanced towards the door.

'What is it?' he asked.

'I feel uncomfortable with …*him* staying over.'

'Why, because he's done time?'

'Yes! And with good reason!'

'Keep it down! He's only next door.'

Veronica sighed and shook her head.

'He's my brother. I know he's always been dependent on me. But what else am I supposed to do? Say no? He's been nice since coming out of jail. He's a changed man—I strongly believe that!'

'And you've been even nicer to him!'

'Darling,' replied Alberto shaking his head and gently stroking her hair—encouraging her to change the subject.

It suddenly dawned on her that he had a tough day ahead, and if anyone needed comforting, it was him—not to mention that they'd be up most of the night, feeding stacks of cash through the machine.

'Did you hear that?' asked Veronica.

'Hear what?'

'I thought I heard a noise.'

'What kind of noise?'

'Like a door closing.'

Alberto didn't seem too interested. He waited for the next batch of notes to be counted before he sealed them in a small plastic bag and placed it into the small brown leather suitcase.

'It's probably Juan,' he said.

'Yes, you're probably right,' she replied, acknowledging that she wasn't used to having guests stay overnight.

She then looked at the suitcase. 'You're actually giving it away? I thought you liked that one.'

'Actually, this one's Juan's. Both were gifts from Uncle Alex years ago. He gave one to me and one to Juan. Juan said he wanted to help somehow so gave me his to carry the ransom money.'

'Why would he do that? Why is he being extra nice?' questioned Veronica.

'You're being paranoid again! Sometimes, people change. Plus, like you said before, I've been good to him. Ever since he came out of jail, I've taken care of him!'

Veronica raised her eyebrows, but kept silent. She kept her thoughts to herself. She always thought that both brothers were different from each other—opposite characters. While in her eyes Alberto was trustworthy, a true gentleman and always kept his word, she couldn't say the same thing about Juan. He was cunning, fake and even tried to flirt with her on occasion. But she had always kept her distance.

By 3:38 AM, the counting was completed. All the cash was in plastic folders and inside the suitcase, ready to be traded. It was time to get Daniela back.

35

THE Inspector sat at his office desk, trying to picture how the night's events would unfold. He then did something that he barely ever did—he prayed. He begged for Daniela's safe return. He prayed she wasn't hurt and he prayed for her not to get hurt.

He also did something else that he didn't often do—not as much as he wanted to anyway. He called his parents who lived in North London. His mother was always the one who called him. Sometimes, if his father was feeling social or if he had a couple of drinks, she would pass the phone over to him. But Kean hardly ever had time to call due to his busy schedule. However, on this occasion, he felt lonely. He spent most of the morning sitting at his desk thinking of Daniela. No one in his life had had such an effect on him as her. Not even Gale Stockyard, who was a long-term girlfriend many years ago. When he found out Gale—who was a primary school teacher—was cheating on him with the Head of Music, Kean ended the relationship feeling extremely hurt, promising himself he'd never get involved seriously again. *That* promise was somehow broken when he had laid eyes on Daniela the evening she had come to the police station. And now the pain was much worse than when he had broken up with Gale.

As he started to dial his parents' home number, the only one that he knew from memory (apart from his own), a withheld number called him. With a deep sigh, he hesitantly answered.

'Well, even I can't make sense of this one,' said X's distorted voice at the other end of the line.

'What do you mean?' asked Kean, surprised.

'The location. How is the kidnapper planning on entering the cathedral grounds with all the security around?'

'I have no idea, but that's what the ransom letter states.'

'The riddle? Something seems a little off.'

'Then what do you suggest? Because I'm lost!' Kean raised his voice in frustration.

'I can see this one has become personal, Inspector. I say go with the ride and see what they have in store. Wait for them to come to you, otherwise you'll be chasing shadows again.'

'I'm not even in charge of the case anymore. So, the final decision isn't up to me,' replied Kean.

'*That* is the main reason why I called you. As they say, *too many cooks spoil the broth*. So, you'll be giving the briefing this morning. You're in charge of the case again! And when you look through the paperwork, I'm sure you'll have a clearer picture!'

'But what about Noel— ?'

'I've taken care of Noel.'

Kean fell silent for a second. He could hear X's distorted short sharp breaths, then he heard a door close. 'Oh no, what did you do?' he asked.

The office phone started ringing.

'That will be for you. Good luck, Inspector.'

'Wait! What do you mean I will have a clearer picture!?' asked Kean, but X had already hung up.

Kean answered the office phone. It was Superintendent Lowe.

'Nick?'

'Hello, Superintendent.'

'Noel went home. You're in charge of the case. Make sure you take his notes from O'Leary and prepare for the briefing. You've got an hour!'

'Why did Noel go home?'

'Bad stomach. He couldn't keep away from the toilet,' Lowe chuckled to himself.

When he got off the phone, Kean couldn't help but think that X must have gone to the police station to slip a laxative into Noel's coffee. He wasn't sure if he appreciated X's gesture, but there was hardly any time left. The MP was going to be at the cathedral tonight, and he needed to be caught. And due to his cunningness, Kean knew that it wouldn't be easy. His priority was Daniela's safety—something he was sure Noel would overlook if it meant catching the MP.

Abruptly, he jumped up from his chair and hurried to the front desk, running past Constable Reading and heading for the front door. He rushed outside and scanned the area, seeking anyone in a long cream-coloured coat and a black hat. But there was hardly anyone around that remotely resembled X.

''Everything okay, Inspector?' asked Reading, when he walked back in.

'Yes—everything's fine.'

'If you don't mind me saying so, you seem a little flustered.'

'Constable, have you seen anyone hurrying out in the last couple of minutes? Male—similar height as you?'

Reading thought for a moment and shook his head. 'Not to my knowledge, Inspector. Shall I sound the alarm?'

'No! That won't be necessary.'

<h1 style="text-align:center">36</h1>

THE sergeants looked relieved to see that Kean was in charge of the case once again when he walked into the room for the morning briefing.

'So, what did you do to Inspector Griffith?' joked Rickson, receiving a few laughs from the others.

'I didn't do anything. Can we concentrate on the meeting?' said Kean, who couldn't resist a smile himself.

There was a knock at the door. It was Pamela, holding a thin paper file in her hand.

'Sorry to disturb the meeting, but here are the results you asked for,' she said, walking up to Kean and handing the file to him before turning and whispering *sorry* again to the sergeants, then hurrying out of the room.

The Inspector opened the file and peered at the report inside.

'What is it, Inspector?' asked O'Leary when seeing the expression on Kean's face.

'It's confirmation that the second amputated finger belongs to a different person from the first. Also male. This one appears to be older. Which makes sense as Alberto

Flores has already confirmed in his statement that it belongs to a Ricardo Matos. Someone he hired to keep an eye out for Daniela.'

'Why didn't he mention Matos before?' asked Mary Phillipson, one of the sergeants.

'If Alberto Flores kept this from us, God knows what other secrets he's keeping,' said Rickson.

'He didn't know that Matos followed Daniela when she was kidnapped,' Kean said. 'But there's more to this pathology report.'

The room fell silent.

'Mato's amputated finger had a ring. Apart from Mato's, there are three more fingerprints on the ring. One belongs to Julie West, and the other to James Sturridge. But the question is: who does the third one belong to?'

'Ron Blates?' asked Sergeant Phillipson.

'Incorrect. The reason why I didn't mention Ron Blates is that there is another report here. The first amputated finger belongs to him. The fingerprints from the amputated finger are a perfect match to the ones found on Ron's laptop.'

The sergeants listened in curious silence.

'I will get to the third fingerprint later, but first, I want to discuss the description of the postman that Juan Flores gave,' continued Kean.

He then turned and glanced at the artist's impression of the postman. And then the picture of him next to it that Jamie's mother had given.

'There is no question about it that James Sturridge was the fake postman,' said O'Leary.

'It's uncanny. It's definitely him,' added Rickson.

The Inspector had seen many portraits of burglars, rapists, and various other criminals throughout his career, but none of them were this accurate.

He turned and glanced at the sergeants.

'If I remember correctly, the security cameras were tampered with too,' he said.

'Yes, Jamie must have somehow managed to delete them,' suggested O'Leary.

'But how? Unless, somehow, he managed to enter the house,' said Sergeant Phillipson.

'Jamie Sturridge was never at the house,' said Kean, his voice cold and emotionless.

The room became quiet once again, as the sergeants waited for more, but Kean just stared into space, deep in thought.

'What do you mean?' asked O'Leary impatiently, breaking the silence, on the edge of his seat.

'How's that possible? The portrait proves that he *was* there!' said Sergeant Phillipson, pointing to the board behind Kean.

'No postman was seen around the area at that time. The only person that claims to have seen one is Juan Flores, who supposedly took the package from him. His description of Jamie Sturridge was so accurate that he must have spent a lot more time with him. If you only saw someone briefly, would you remember small details like a tiny mole at the edge of their eye or slight scarring beneath the chin? So, going back to the deleted camera recordings. Sturridge never went into the house …but Juan Flores did!'

The room remained silent.

'Ladies and gentlemen, I believe we have found *The Silent Killer*, or shall I say, the *Mexican Politician*!' added Kean.

'Inspector, with all respect, that's a shocking accusation! There'll need to be solid evidence before we can even start pointing fingers at Alberto's brother!' gasped O'Leary.

'The third set of fingerprints on the ring were also on the package that Juan claims he took from the postman,' said Kean, pulling out another piece of paper from the forensics file and turning it around to expose the report to the sergeants. 'And guess what? They are Juan's …the mastermind behind these killings and the kidnapping of his niece—Daniela Flores!'

Everyone in the room listened in shock.

'We must inform Alberto Flores immediately before anyone else gets hurt,' O'Leary cut the silence.

'Alberto is on his way down from London with the money, but it is thought that Juan stayed behind with Veronica Flores. The Met have the Flores mansion surrounded. They won't enter until Daniela is safely returned,' said Kean.

'And how about the bag with the cash inside, Inspector?' asked O'Leary.

'When Alberto arrives in his hotel room, a plain-clothes officer will go and fit the tracker into the bag.'

There was a loud knock on the door. It was Constable Steven Reading. He walked up to Kean and spoke softly, unsure whether the information that he was about to give needed to be shared directly with the Inspector first.

'We just had an anonymous call from a man.'

'What did he say?'

'That all the electricity should to be cut off in and around the cathedral this evening. Apart from Alberto Flores, no one else should enter the garden. Otherwise, Daniela will be killed.'

'Did you trace the call?' sighed Kean.

'Yes, Inspector, we got a direct location from a payphone in Tilmanstone.'

The Inspector stopped and turned towards Reading.

Tilmanstone? 'That's—'

'Where Jamie Sturridge's mother lives,' cut in Reading.

Kean looked at Reading, surprised how he knew that.

'Exactly,' he answered.

'Now if you excuse me, Inspector, I have to go back and keep guard of the front line,' smiled Reading.

'Yes of course. Thank you, Constable,' Kean said, then turned his attention back on the sergeants. 'Phillipson, O'Leary! Let's pay Tilmanstone a visit!'

37

WHEN the dilapidated phone box was finally located, it started to rain. The place was secluded, and although there were a couple of houses down the road and an old scrapyard at the other side of the wall, much of the surrounding area was open fields and farmland.

'He could be hiding in one of those houses,' Sergeant Philipson suggested, rubbing her hands warm while squinting towards the row of houses down the road.

'O'Leary, take a look at the scrapyard. Philipson, you search the field for any tracks, while I go check out those houses. Someone *must've* seen him!'

O'Leary gave Kean an odd look. 'When you say *him*, Inspector, I gather you mean Jamie Sturridge?'

'As Juan is supposedly in London and it was a man that made the call, it only leaves Sturridge.'

It took Kean a good ten minutes to reach the first house and just as he was about to ring the doorbell, O'Leary called.

'Inspector, I think you should take a look at this!' he said in a horrified voice.

Kean hurried back up the road, the rain falling more heavily now as he ran around the wall and into the scrapyard, Sergeant Mary Philipson following him from behind.

Upon entering the gates, Kean had to do a double-take. O'Leary was knelt between what appeared to be two bodies, both lying lifelessly in a pool of blood, soaking from the rain—he checked one of them for a pulse, and then the other before getting up and shaking his head disappointedly. Kean and Philipson were now both standing beside him transfixed on the two dead bodies on the ground.

Kean recognised Julie by the reddish colour of her hair and her dark red puffer jacket. Her face was swollen and bloodstained, a bullet hole in the middle of her forehead which was still fresh. Next to her was Jamie Sturridge—also shot in the forehead the same way as Julie. Whoever did this was very accurate with their aim—they must have been standing some distance away judging by the size of the bullet holes. This was the work of a professional.

'I already called for backup,' O'Leary whispered sharply, receiving a nod of approval from Kean.

Sergeant Philipson was just about to say something but Kean and O'Leary both gestured for her to *hush*, as Kean pointed to the warehouse ahead.

The killer could be close by!

The Inspector then turned and stared at the small cabin while removing his Glock 26 pistol from its holster. He signalled for them to wait while he went to check inside.

'I'll back you up,' whispered O'Leary, receiving a thumbs up from Kean.

Apart from a desk and a small room with a dirty mattress on the floor, the place was empty. He walked out and headed straight towards the warehouse. O'Leary and Philipson followed.

Making minimal noise, Kean slowly slid the warehouse door open just wide enough for them to pass through. The place was dark, the smell rancid.

'Police!' called Kean, tightly gripping the pistol.

There was no answer, so he continued walking cautiously, with the others following him closely from behind. For more visibility, Sergeant Mary Philipson shone her phone's light over Kean's shoulder. After making it past the large stack of boxes, the first thing Kean noticed was a piece of rope tied to a railing at the far end. There was a bowl of water and a sandwich scattered over the floor.

'Someone wasn't feeling hungry,' whispered O'Leary.

Kean walked up to the rope and saw something reflecting from the phone's light. It was a strand of long black hair. He held it closer and carefully examined it.

'Daniela,' he breathed.

'Look, Inspector!' exclaimed Philipson, pointing to the blood-stained floor nearby.

'We need to make sure—' Kean started but then got distracted by the sound of multiple sirens echoing outside.

'Forensics will have their work cut out,' O'Leary cut in.

'The whole area needs to be searched!' Kean said, kneeling and taking a closer look at splats of blood on the floor.

Just as the CO19 team blasted in, the Inspector felt his phone vibrating in his pocket. It was Superintendent Lowe.

'Just had confirmation from London that Juan Flores isn't in the house,' he said. 'He must have left before Alberto this morning.'

'Makes sense,' replied Kean, scanning the warehouse wide-eyed while making his way out. 'He's in Tilmanstone. He killed Julie West and Jamie Sturridge. Daniela must be with him.'

'Let's try to track them down before they reach the cathedral tonight. Have all the entrance points into the city checked. Every car, bus, bike, train, and pedestrian!'

'Yes, Superintendent,' replied Kean, his stomach churning as he walked past the lifeless bodies of Julie and Jamie.

38

BLINDFOLDED and with her hands tied behind her back, Daniela was forced by Juan into the boot of his car, and he then started to drive.

She could have sworn someone else was inside with her—but tried not to think about it. The drive didn't seem long and when the boot was opened again, she welcomed the clean fresh air into her lungs while droplets of rain fell onto her face.

Juan forced her back out of the boot and onto a gravel surface. They walked for a while until the ground eventually became smoother. He then rang a doorbell and it wasn't long before she heard someone open the door.

'You promised that the police wouldn't come here asking questions!' gasped a man with a hoarse voice.

He sounded irritated and judging from his tone, Daniela guessed he was elderly.

'Let's discuss that later. Can we come in first?' asked Juan calmly.

'Yeah,' grunted the man hesitantly before letting them in.

'It was a bold move, giving Jamie's name.'

'They had evidence with my name and number on it!' explained the man.

'We're scared they'll be back asking more questions!' cut in a lady's squeaky voice.

'You have nothing to worry about. They're busy faffing around at the cathedral. Plus, you earned their trust by giving them Jamie's name.'

Daniela felt Juan's hand under her arm strongly tugging her into the warmth of the house. She would have let out a yell if it wasn't for the damn tape stuck over her mouth. She had missed the feeling of cosiness. Being in the freezing warehouse for days made her unwell. Her chest was full, and because of the tape, she kept coughing through her nostrils, which was torturous.

'She's sick. I'll take her up to the room,' said the lady.

'And how about the other one?' asked the man.

'Go ahead,' said Juan approvingly.

'So, when can we have our share?' Daniela heard the man ask, as the lady escorted her up some stairs to what she only imagined was a spare bedroom.

'I have it right here, inside the case,' replied Juan.

Daniela shook her head in horror as she tried to warn them that Juan would shoot them, but she started to cough uncontrollably again.

'She needs cough syrup,' said the lady.

'I don't care what she needs, as long as she's out of the bloody way until tonight!'

The lady escorted her inside the room and onto the side of a bed.

'Please, at least take the blindfold off!' begged Daniela, moaning under the tape, but the lady ignored her. Not that she would have understood what she had said.

She then sensed the other end of the mattress being pushing down as if someone else was sitting on the bed with her. The door slammed shut. Daniela felt petrified.

'Hello? Who's there?' she tried to ask, trembling.

There was no reply, just heavy breathing.

Time passed—she dosed off and abruptly awoke up again—not knowing if it was night or day, or what day of the week, or even what month it was. The breathing continued, like a saw cutting through wood. Sometimes it eased and at other times it grew sharper, heavier. Daniela got used to the sound of it and there were times her ears even cut it out completely.

She thought of the moment her uncle had materialised in the darkness of the warehouse.

'How?' she had asked him in disbelief, unable to project her voice.

He looked frail and had aged since she had seen him last before he went to jail.

'Hello, mijita,' he said with a grin.

She felt a tear slowly running down her face, 'Why?'

He rested the metal case on the ground and clicked it open. Reaching inside, he removed a large syringe, and with a grunt, looked briefly over at Ron. He then cast his attention back to Daniela.

'Your father. He got it all didn't he? The luxury life, the big houses, the fancy cars. Fair enough! He even married the girl that I once loved. So be it. But what hurt the most was him selling me out! He destroyed my life! Took my share of the will. Fucking setting me up! Getting me put away, you know? Don't get me wrong. This is nothing personal against you—mijita. But everything has consequences. And now the time has come for *him* to face them.'

Daniela could see through her uncle's charm and manipulating attitude—the two traits that pulled the wool over so many people's eyes, ruining their lives.

'No,' she trembled, shaking her head.

'And do you know what the worst part is?' added Juan. '*He* doesn't even realise what he's done!'

'My father has been nothing but good to you. He helped you!'

'Helped me? With my money? Well, guess what, I'm taking what is rightly mine at last. No hard feelings. You're his most valuable thing, so this is the only way I could get his attention,' he said, kneeling next to Ron, pulling back his sleeve, then jabbing the needle into his arm while injecting the substance inside the syringe.

After, he put the blindfold over Daniela, placing black tape over her mouth. The last thing she saw was his crazy stare. Everything suddenly made sense. Whoever she got close to was killed. She was even labelled a killer, denting her father's pride. Juan had carefully planned everything before her kidnapping. The only person who truly believed that she was innocent was Kean. She prayed that he would find her and save her from this monstrous nightmare.

The thing that scared her the most was the uncertainty of what was going to happen to her. Juan had said something about the cathedral to the man downstairs. Julie had also mentioned something to her about it. Why did Juan bring her here, and what was happening at the cathedral tonight?

The doorbell rang. Gathering up what little strength she had in her, she tried to scream through the tape, but it was to no avail. Then she heard something that caused her heart to beat faster. It was Kean's voice. She couldn't make out what he was saying, but she was sure it was him by the tone of his voice.

Desperately, she started to stamp her feet on the floor, but it didn't seem to work. She managed to get herself up, but after a step or two, stumbled to the floor. It wasn't long before she heard the front door closing.

'No!' she sobbed with a muffled voice, feeling furious and broken that he didn't check upstairs.

Suddenly, the door to the room opened, and she heard footsteps approaching. Someone pulled her up from the floor and threw her back onto the bed. Immense pain shot across her left cheek.

'You fucking bitch! You almost ruined everything!' blasted Juan's angry voice.

He then walked back out, slamming the bedroom door behind him.

After some more time had passed, there was screaming from downstairs. It was the lady. An eerie silence followed. She could only imagine what had just occurred. Juan must have shot them both. The only sound that she could hear was her own heartbeat pounding hard against her chest. Even the heavy breathing from the other side of the bed had come to a stop. She battled hard to free her wrists from the tightly bound rope, but the more she struggled, the weaker she felt.

A while later, the door swung open again. Someone walked up to her and abruptly tore the tape from her mouth. It burnt like mad, so she let out a scream until she felt something cold and sharp pressing up against her left temple— followed by a metallic click.

'If you don't eat, mijita, I will blow your beautiful brains out,' said Juan's voice in a way that was both polite and chilling at the same time.

He then pressed something against her mouth. It smelled pleasant. With the fear and hunger getting the better of her, she took a small bite. It was something flat and soft with a moist, sweet top. It took a while for her to register what it was that she was churning in her mouth, ultimately realising that it was bread with butter. She felt comforted after not eating for so long.

'That's right, you must build up your energy for tonight,' he whispered.

Summoning up all her courage, she asked, 'What's happening tonight?'

She felt a cup pressing against her lips.

'Have some water,' he said, ignoring the question.

She did.

'It's almost time,' he said, placing the tape back over her mouth after she'd finished drinking.

39

ALBERTO angrily stomped towards the cathedral. The wind was so strong that he fought hard to keep moving forward as bullets of rain whipped down on his face. The pain was nothing compared to the anguish he was going through emotionally. He felt betrayed. He couldn't accept the fact that his brother had kidnapped Daniela—it made him nauseous to think that Juan had slept at his house the night before and also that he had stayed alone with his wife.

He welcomed the warmness of the bulletproof vest wrapped around his chest beneath his shirt. It turned out to be a wise decision to wear the dark green hunter's coat that he'd purchased from a store in Central London many years ago. It was still as good as new, and he still remembered the store assistant telling him—while offering him a glass of champagne on a golden tray—that the coat was guaranteed to last for many years. For the price Alberto ended up paying at the time, he had bloody well hoped so. And the store assistant turned out to be correct. On this chilly night, Alberto was particularly grateful that the coat's thermal hood kept his ears warm.

Earlier, he had had a brief chat with Inspector Nicolas Kean, who mentioned that snipers would be concealed on the roofs of nearby buildings. He tried to spot them, but the driving rain made visibility difficult.

He arrived at the cloister garden. Even though the surrounding area was heavily guarded, the place was secluded and dark—the power was turned off, just as requested on the ransom note—which gave the garden a ghostly feel with shadows playing on the surrounding stone arches.

The flag on top of the tower flapped noisily in the wind. Taking in a deep breath and turning on his phone's torch, Alberto continued through, heading towards the tower side next to the main building of the cathedral.

Amazed at Juan's cunningness, he stopped and gently laid the suitcase on the ground. He was actually returning his suitcase back to him with ten million pounds in cash inside. How on earth did he think he was going to get away with it? The area was heavily guarded—*No way out!*

The tracking chip was as small as the nail on his little finger—without fully opening the suitcase's zip, the plain-clothes officer was able to drop it through the gap. So, if Juan did manage to somehow get away, he would be tracked down fast.

How could he do this to me!? Alberto numbly asked himself.

The time on his phone's screen read 20:58. It was almost time. He just wanted to get it over with.

Angrily, he brought up Juan's name and pressed call. After a couple of rings, Juan answered.

'You bastard!' Alberto spat when he heard his voice.

'And what does that make you, brother?' replied Juan smugly.

'You better not have hurt her!'

'You think I'd physically hurt my dear niece? I even eliminated the person who tried to kill her with carbon monoxide!'

'Where are you—?' Alberto stopped and focused on a shadow emerging from one of the arches on the other side of the garden.

'I'm surprised you didn't work it out sooner,' said Juan.

With his limited vision, Alberto saw that there were two figures. He assumed the male one was Juan—with his hand over Daniela's mouth. In his other hand, he wildly waved a gun.

'Daniela! Stay calm, baby! Daddy's here for you!'

Daniela moaned loudly, her mouth covered.

'The money's here!' Alberto called out at him angrily. 'Let her go!'

Juan didn't reply. It seemed as though he was struggling as he wildly waved the gun. So much so that he and Daniela almost both tumbled over.

Suddenly, the gun fired, aimed towards Daniela's head. Then there was another loud bang, then another, causing Alberto to drop to the ground and shelter himself behind one of the benches. Then, everything suddenly went silent, with ringing echoing in his ears.

When he looked up, at first, he couldn't locate the whereabouts of Juan and Daniela, but then he noticed them lying on the ground.

'NO! DANIELA! MY BABY!' he cried, forcing himself up.

All of a sudden, the place was swarming with armed police. Inspector Nicolas Kean ran past him, briefly stopping to ask Alberto if he was okay. Trembling with shock, he just looked back at him blankly.

The Inspector was one of the first to arrive at the scene. Juan and Daniela now became visible under newly illuminated spotlights, which bathed the entire courtyard in light. Juan had a black balaclava over his face. His left hand was duct-taped over Daniela's mouth, and a pistol was taped to his other hand—index finger over the trigger—as he lay on the ground without flinching. Daniela lay trapped under Juan's body, tears running down her face. Relief washed over Kean when he noticed that she had not been hit. He rushed to help her, but a hand grabbed onto his arm from behind as the bomb removal unit pushed past him to perform a check. He noticed it was O'Leary that had stopped him from going forward.

'Thanks,' whispered Kean.

'Sometimes, Inspector, it's easy to lose yourself.'

'All clear!' called the unit leader after a minute, allowing Kean and O'Leary to pass through, followed by more police.

'What's with the tape?' asked O'Leary, baffled.

'No idea,' Kean replied, just as confused as O'Leary.

He kneeled down next to Daniela, who had duct-tape running across her face with Juan's hand heavily taped across her mouth, and gave her a sympathetic look.

'Hey,' he breathed.

Although she couldn't talk, she blinked her eyes, looking relieved to see him. *Hey*.

He removed his Swiss Army knife and started cutting through the tape, firstly managing to free the hand from over her mouth.

'Inspector,' said O'Leary, looking down at Juan, who had a couple of armed officers surrounding him with rifles aimed as he lay in a pool of blood.

'Go ahead,' replied Kean, working the Swiss Army knife's scissors across the tape, trying hard not to pierce Daniela's skin.

Ambulance sirens echoed around the garden as O'Leary kneeled and delicately removed the balaclava as everyone looked on in shock.

'I fucking knew it!' echoed Alberto's irritated voice from behind. 'Juan is too much of a coward to come here in person!'

Kean focused on the man lying lifelessly across Daniela who had his hand across her mouth. It was Ron.

O'Leary realised that he couldn't check for a pulse as Ron had been hit on the side of the neck and had blood spraying out of his jugular. He quickly removed his coat and applied pressure to it.

'Where's the ambulance!' he called.

Finally, Kean managed to free Daniela from the tape. She sat up, tightly put her arms around him and started to cry. She looked thin and pale. Alberto pushed his way in and hugged his daughter too, before the paramedics came to take her to get checked at the hospital. Ron was pronounced dead. They placed a sheet over him and wheeled him to a separate ambulance.

'I'm sorry,' cried Alberto, stroking Daniela's hair. 'I'm so sorry!'

Kean suddenly began to panic as alarm bells started ringing in his head. Why would Juan do such a thing and not take the ransom money? Or had he already taken it somehow? No—Alberto was tightly holding onto it.

'Mr Flores, you'll need to bring that to the station,' said Kean.

'You can take your tracker back too.' Alberto nodded.

For the first time since meeting him, Kean saw a relieved look on his face.

But the Inspector was far from relieved. He wouldn't relax until Juan had been caught.

40

WHEN Kean entered the police station with Alberto and O'Leary, Constable John Dawes was sitting at the front desk. He looked up and gave them a friendly smile.

'Good work tonight.'

'That's debatable, Constable. An innocent man was shot dead by our unit. And there's still a killer out on the loose. Superintendent Lowe is demanding an urgent report on the matter.'

'Yes, but at least Miss Flores is safe now.'

'Indeed,' Kean raised a relieved smile.

He then stopped. 'Are you on a double shift?'

'Apparently, Constable Reading couldn't make it in today—for personal reasons.'

'I see. That's unusual for him. He practically lives in this place.'

Kean, Alberto and O'Leary, who was now carrying the suitcase with the ransom money, carried on through to the Inspector's office. Once inside, Kean took the case from O'Leary and rested it on the table. Alberto noticed that the orange leather had now turned brown after getting soaked from the rain.

'I know you want to be with Daniela, but until Juan has been caught, the case must stay here,' explained Kean, delicately unzipping it.

'We're still at a loss as to why he released Daniela without taking the ransom,' added O'Leary.

Alberto shook his head. 'I really don't know.'

'You see, we don't understand the motive behind it,' explained Kean, opening the case.

Inside was a duvet with a transparent plastic sheet wrapped around it. All three men looked on blankly without saying a word.

Kean reached down slowly, removed the duvet and looked inside. Apart from the tracking chip, the case was empty.

'So, where's the cash?' he asked.

Alberto shook his head in disbelief.

'Did you think you'd get away with trading a duvet for your daughter?' asked O'Leary coldly.

'No! The money was in here! I swear! This doesn't make any sense! Where's my money!?' gasped Alberto, sounding as if he was on the verge of having a nervous breakdown.

'That's a question we hope you can answer,' said Kean, removing the tracker from the case and examining it while twisting it around with his fingers.

Alberto stopped for a moment and then flopped down on the chair, covering his face with his hands. He started taking deep breaths, trying to calm himself. Kean and O'Leary shot each other a look.

'He swapped the cases,' Alberto said with a muffled voice, his hands still over his face.

'What was that?' asked Kean.

'Juan already had the case with the money! That's why he never showed up at the cathedral! He used it as a distraction!'

'How did he get the case that had the money?'

The two policemen listened in shock as Alberto Flores explained that Juan had exactly the same case and must have swapped them while he was staying at Alberto's house.

'And you didn't think to check the money for an entire day?' asked O'Leary.

'I wasn't going to expose what's inside the case! I've been out most of the day. The cash was wrapped in plastic bags. I kept hearing the plastic so didn't think it was necessary to check,' said Alberto, as he disappointedly stared at the plastic wrapped duvet.

Kean and O'Leary were silent, feeling defeated that they had managed to let Juan get away.

'I kept hearing the plastic,' repeated Alberto like a broken record.

'Maybe Daniela can help us. She might have some idea where Juan is headed,' suggested O'Leary.

'It's a long shot, but let's talk to Daniela before he goes too far. O'Leary, alert all the other stations around Kent. And I mean *Everyone* needs to be on alert. We're running out of time!' said Kean, grabbing his coat and heading for the door.

He then stopped and turned to Alberto. 'I'll give you a ride to the hospital.'

As they were walking past the front desk, Constable Dawes drew Kean's attention to the fact that Reading wouldn't be in for a while.

'How come?' Kean asked.

'I heard that he's in hospital, Inspector. Walked into A&E not so long ago. Apparently, he's fractured his arm. Fell over while cycling.'

'Poor Reading. What was he doing cycling in this weather?'

'No idea,' shrugged Dawes. 'He's always been a bit eccentric. By the way ...are you going to the hospital, Inspector?'

'Yes I am. Why do you ask?'

'I was wondering if you could do me a favour. Reading forgot his keys here. Would you be able to take them to him?'

'Of course,' said Kean, taking the bunch of keys from Dawes and shoving them into his jacket pocket.

41

IT was potentially going to be most extensive manhunt Kean had ever encountered since joining the force—even larger than the previous one for *The Silent Killer*, he thought. Presumably, it would be more straightforward because he now had a face and a name.

Alberto quietly sat at the back of Kean's car with his hands on his knees and in deep thought, possibly thinking the same thing as Kean. *Will Juan be caught?* Although Daniela was safe, Kean thought Alberto must have been desperate to get his ten million back. Just as they turned onto Old Dover Road, Kean received a call from X.

'Location A251. Approximately a mile after The Frog and Crown pub. He couldn't have gone far,' buzzed X's distorted voice, which sounded somewhat different this time. It sounded strained, as if he was in pain.

'What's going on?' asked Kean, but X had already hung up. 'Shit!'

He glanced at Alberto through the rear-view mirror, who was blankly looking back at him.

'Sorry,' Kean said before doing a sharp U-turn, greeted by an angry blowing of horns.

'What the hell is going on!?' gasped Alberto with a shaky voice.

'We just had a tip-off,' replied Kean, pressing hard on the gas.

Twenty minutes later, flashing blue lights were visible down the road from the Frog and Crown, a secluded pub located in a wooded area on the A251. They drove past a diversion sign and continued down the road. Eventually, they approached a parked police car shining its headlights on a black BMW that had crashed into a tractor, which looked as though it had been pulling out onto the main road.

The front of the BMW was severely damaged, with its headlights smashed, its bumper on the ground and the airbag deployed. The tractor had a huge dent on its side, but was in no way as badly damaged as the car. Kean parked behind the police vehicle and turned off the engine.

'Oh God!' exclaimed Alberto from the back when he saw the crash scene.

'You recognise the car?' Kean asked him.

'Yes, it's the one Juan had rented.'

They both rushed out and were confronted by a police officer who shone his torch at their faces, blinding them.

'You can't be here,' he warned.

'Inspector Nicolas Kean,' said Kean, flashing his badge at him while raising his other hand to block the torch's light.

'Inspector,' nodded the officer approvingly, letting them pass.

'Any casualties?' asked Kean.

'Hard to say. Both the vehicles have been abandoned.'

'Interesting.'

'We found a black suitcase in the boot of the car. It has some clothes in.'

'Definitely Juan,' said Alberto.

Kean walked up to the BMW. He took out his phone and turned on its torch. The passenger door was open with trails of blood splattered over the ground leading towards the woods.

'Search the woods!' he called out at the other policemen.

Approximately an hour later, Juan—with blood all over his face—was tracked down about half a mile away inside the wooded area, barely crawling, with a pistol in one hand and the orange suitcase clenched tightly in the other. Although he was aware that the police had him surrounded, he still did his best to keep going as far as his injured knee allowed.

'PUT YOUR HANDS UP AND THROW DOWN YOUR WEAPON!' one of the officers called out to him.

Juan hesitated for a second and then struggled a bit more, not accepting defeat—but then slowly turned and faced the police, kneeling upright and raising his hands. Then suddenly, without hesitation, he pressed the pistol onto his temple and squeezed the trigger.

It looked almost theatrical, as there was hardly a sound. There was no loud bang—just a short sharp pop from the pistol's silencer. It wasn't until much later that it occurred to the Inspector that *The Silent Killer* had lived up to his name and taken his own life silently.

However, a sibling will always be a sibling: Alberto screamed out in horror, ran towards his little brother, and held him in his arms, ignoring the suitcase with the ten million lying on the ground next to him.

Kean walked back to investigate the tractor. Its owner had been located at a nearby farmhouse, but he knew nothing of the incident. What was more shocking was that he still had the tractor's keys in his possession. The tractor had been hotwired.

42

DANIELA was looking better and even managed to raise a smile when Kean walked into the ward with a bouquet of pink lilies that he'd purchased from the hospital shop. As he handed them over to her, their hands made contact—he then leaned down and softly pressed his lips against hers. Gently, they kissed for a while—getting lost in their own world. A sudden emotion flooded over her. Her eyes became watery.

I never thought I'd see him again, she thought.

She looked deep into his soulful eyes and was certain that he felt the same.

Fortunately, the ward wasn't overcrowded, although there was still that distinct smell of disinfectant that most wards had.

'Missed you,' she said softly.

'Me too,' he replied.

'They said they're going to keep me in overnight.'

'Sorry to hear that.'

'I'm not. This place is a luxury compared to where I was living the last couple of days,' she smiled, wiping her tears.

Although it had been more than a couple of days, Kean didn't say anything. He just returned her smile and breathed. 'It's good to have you back.'

'It's good to be back.'

'Did you eat anything?'

'Their vegetable soup is surprisingly good.'

'*Hospital soup* and *good* don't unusually belong in the same sentence,' chuckled Kean, happy to see her upbeat after everything she'd been through.

'Hi,' Daniela said, looking over Kean's shoulder.

Alberto and Veronica—who had just come down from London—were standing behind him.

'Thank you, Inspector,' said Alberto, his arm over his wife's shoulder.

Veronica looked at Daniela and turned her attention to Kean. 'You're always welcome to come visit us whenever you are in London.'

Daniela rolled her eyes and smiled, as if to say '*Mum!*'

'Oh, darling!' she cried, walking over to her daughter and giving her a tight squeeze.

Kean left the Flores family and headed down the corridor. He'd be back to see how Daniela was doing later. In the meantime, he had one more ward to visit.

On the way to the ward where Reading was staying, Kean took the keys out from his pocket and casually examined them. Suddenly, he stopped cold, and his heart skipped a beat—he could hardly breathe. The keyring was a silver cross, with the initials SR engraved on it—the same one he had seen hanging out of X's coat pocket at The Cathedral Café. He realised that it wasn't a cross but an X. Suddenly, everything started to make perfect sense. How else would X have so much information and knowledge about Kean's every move? Constable *Stephen Reading* didn't get injured falling off his bicycle; he got hurt because he was the one who pulled out onto the road with the tractor, causing Juan's rented car to crash into it. He didn't have to run out of the police station after slipping a laxative into Noel's coffee. He only had to go and sit back at the front desk—because Constable Reading *was* X.

He was lying in bed with the right side of his face badly bruised and his right arm covered in a full plaster cast. Kean walked up to him and stood next to his bed. All the divider curtains in the ward were open apart from the ones at the end, which were partly drawn with an old lady dozing off in the cubicle.

'How're you holding up?' he asked Reading.

'I've had better days.'

Kean hesitated for a moment.

'I know who you are,' he whispered, handing Reading the keyring.

'I was wondering when you'd work it out.'

'So, what now?'

'I'm retiring. From now on, you'll have to fight your own battles. I'm handing in my notice to work tomorrow.'

Kean nodded and sighed. 'I guess it was going to happen someday. Can we meet at The Cathedral Café next week so I can pay you your commission—'

Reading raised his free hand. 'How about this time, you get me a coffee instead.'

Kean smiled. 'Why not?'

'Maybe Miss Flores can join us too.'

'Maybe,' replied Kean and started making his way out of the ward. Then he stopped and turned back.

'Constable?'

'Yes?'

'Thank you. I could have never have done it without you.'

'It was a team effort. I hope the tractor wasn't too badly damaged,' Reading smiled.